FINDING FORTUNE

ALSO BY DELIA RAY

• • • • •

*Behind the Blue and Gray: The Soldier's
Life in the Civil War*

Ghost Girl: A Blue Ridge Mountain Story

Singing Hands

Here Lies Linc

FINDING FORTUNE

DELIA RAY

MARGARET FERGUSON BOOKS

FARRAR STRAUS GIROUX
NEW YORK

Farrar Straus Giroux Books for Young Readers
175 Fifth Avenue, New York 10010

Printed in the United States of America by
R. R. Donnelley & Sons Company, Harrisonburg, Virginia
First edition, 2015
1   3   5   7   9   10   8   6   4   2

mackids.com

Library of Congress Cataloging-in-Publication Data
Ray, Delia.
    Finding Fortune / Delia Ray. — First edition.
        pages cm
    Summary: Angry with her mother, twelve-year-old runaway Ren finds
an unusual boardinghouse in a nearby ghost town, Fortune, where she meets
some interesting people and learns of a forgotten treasure from when the
town was famous for buttons made of Mississippi River shells.
    ISBN 978-0-374-30065-4 (hardback)
    ISBN 978-0-374-30067-8 (e-book)
    [1. Boardinghouses—Fiction.   2. Lost and found possessions—Fiction.
3. Family problems—Fiction.   4. Runaways—Fiction.   5. Mystery and
detective stories.]   I. Title.

PZ7.R2101315Fin 2015
[Fic]—dc23

                                                                2014042436

Farrar Straus Giroux Books for Young Readers may be purchased for business
or promotional use. For information on bulk purchases please contact Macmillan
Corporate and Premium Sales Department at (800) 221-7945 x5442 or by email
at specialmarkets@macmillan.com.

For Matt—
My Lucky Charm

FINDING FORTUNE

ONE

FORTUNE, OR WHAT'S LEFT OF IT, is only a few miles from my house. *Mis*-Fortune, people call it around here. *Mis*-Fortune on the *Miss*-issippi. That's because it's a ghost town. When you turn onto Front Street, you pass a crooked sign that says:

Welcome to Fortune
Population: ~~128~~ ~~35~~ *12*

My older sister, Nora, and all my friends think Fortune is spooky because weeds are sprouting out of the sidewalks, and the windows on the old brick buildings are boarded up. And nobody has ever seen a single one of those twelve lonely people wandering around. Still, I like it there. Sometimes when I ride my bike over to the Short

Stop to buy candy, I ride a couple of miles farther, just so I can suck on Jolly Ranchers and smell the big, brown river drifting past and cruise up and down the empty streets thinking about how things must have looked when the town was booming.

Dad says if it weren't for Fortune nobody in the old days would have been able to button up their shirts. Buttons used to be made out of shells, he told me, and the Mississippi happened to be knee-deep in the kind of mussels and clams whose shells were perfect for making the strongest, pearliest buttons. But eventually the shells ran dry and somebody came along and invented plastic buttons and the town of Fortune slowly withered away.

One of my favorite old buildings on Front Street has stone columns and a lion's head carved up near the rooftop, with a name and date etched underneath. *McNally and Sons, Established 1901.* I figure Mr. McNally and those sons of his must have been button-makers because the alley behind their building is still filled with piles of shells—all of them punched through with perfectly round holes like pieces of Swiss cheese.

It turned into a habit of mine this past year, riding to Fortune on my bike whenever I was worried about things—whether Dad was keeping safe and whether he and Mom would get back together once he came home from Afghanistan. Dad moved out two months before he left for duty. He loaded a duffel bag of clothes and Old Blue, his hunting dog, into the back of his truck and went to live in Uncle Spence's basement. "Don't worry," he kept saying to Nora and me. "It's only temporary. Your mother and I will work things out."

And I believed him at first—so much that I didn't tell anybody that my mom and dad might be getting a divorce. Not Allison or Kelly. I even refused to admit it to myself. As much as I hated my father going off to war, I decided that his year away would be the thing that fixed my parents' marriage. There were little signs everywhere to prove it. The picture of Dad in his uniform that Mom kept on her dresser. The birthday card she sent to him back in December. I peeked inside while she was searching for stamps to mail it. "I love you," she had written. "Be safe."

I remember how hopeful I felt this past April when I checked the calendar I had hung on my bedroom door and realized Dad would be home in less than a hundred days. "Only ninety-nine more," I chanted on my way out to Fortune that afternoon with my legs pumping like pistons. "Ninety-nine more . . . Ninety-nine more till life goes back to normal again."

I could see it all in my head, like a 3-D movie, as I sped past the tidy farmhouses and the plowed fields—Dad arriving back at the community rec center, marching in with all the other soldiers right on time. His face would light up when he spotted Nora and me in the crowd, wearing our sundresses and holding our banner and balloons. Then he would see Mom standing behind us, and as soon as the commander announced, "Troops dismissed!" we'd all run to meet him and hug and laugh and cry. I must have played that happy-reunion movie in my mind a thousand times since then.

But lately the movie has been changing and I have to squeeze my eyes shut to try and stop it before it gets to the end, to the part where Dad hugs Nora and me, searching the jumble of faces over our shoulders. "Is your mother here?" he whispers, and all we can do is shake our heads no.

On those days, when I can't stop that awful scene from rewinding, I get off my bike in Fortune and sit on the sagging bench in front of McNally and Sons. I stare at the pretty old buildings with their "Keep Out" signs, wondering why things always have to change. Why do people have to move away from perfectly good towns like Fortune? Why do countries have to start wars? And why did a creep like Rick Littleton have to move onto our street and ruin everything right before Dad was due to come home?

When I woke up this morning though, I pushed all my worries about my parents to the back of my mind. The last day of sixth grade had finally arrived and there were more urgent issues to think about—like how to tame my mind-of-its-own hair and what outfit to wear for graduation.

"Why are you wearing *that*?" Mom said when I came downstairs in my fourth change of clothes and two more hair clips than usual. "There's the picnic on the playground after the assembly, remember? You can't run around and play tug-of-war in a dress. Plus I've got to get to work early today, so you'll have to ride your bike to school." She was scurrying around, searching for her car keys. "Go put your khaki shorts back on. They were perfect."

Mom promised to see me at the assembly, but when I filed into the auditorium a few hours later, she still hadn't arrived. Luckily our last name starts with *W*, and she ducked in the side door just in time to see me march across the stage to get my certificate and shake the principal's hand. When Mrs. Adams called me back to the stage a few minutes later to receive the Language Arts award, I could see Mom clapping and hopping up and down like I had just won an Olympic medal.

After the ceremony was over, she gave me a big hug and took a picture of me holding my trophy with its little gold stack of books on top and my entire name—*Renata Jane Winningham*—engraved underneath. But then I noticed Mom checking her watch for the third time.

"What's wrong?" I asked. "Aren't you staying for the picnic?"

"I'm sorry, honey," she said. "It's been a crazy morning at the office. I've got to get right back." She paused. "And I'm afraid I might have to work late tonight too. But you've got the pool party at Allison's this afternoon. Do you think you can stay for dinner once the party's done? I'm sure Carol won't mind."

"What's Nora doing?" I asked.

"She doesn't get off work till seven-thirty."

I sighed. Even though Nora's junior year was winding down, I barely saw her anymore. When she wasn't at school, she was either waitressing at the diner where she had worked since last summer or off somewhere with Alain, her exchange-student boyfriend who was flying back home to Paris in July.

"So what do you think?" Mom said. "Have we got a plan?"

I shrugged, peering around her shoulder. "I guess so," I murmured vaguely. Two teachers were posted at the doorways to the playground, passing out the memory books we had all been waiting for. Through the windows I could see my classmates already hovered over their copies, trading signatures and squealing and laughing as they turned the pages.

Mom gave me one more hug. "Have fun, honey," she said. "I'll see you later tonight, okay?" I nodded, stuck my trophy in my backpack, and ran off to get in line for my memory book.

School let out two hours early for all the graduates and I rode my bike straight to Allison's house. She had invited me and a few other girls over, and we spent the rest of the afternoon floating on rafts in her big, blue-bottomed pool, eating Twizzlers and comparing what the boys had signed in our books. But when five o'clock came and parents began arriving for pickup, I was too embarrassed to ask Mrs. Holman if I could stay. Allison had mentioned that her family was taking her out to dinner to celebrate and I didn't want to be a tagalong.

It wasn't until I was riding home on my bike, breathing in the summery smells of hamburgers on the grill and fresh-cut grass, that I started officially feeling sorry for myself. Here it was my very last day of John Glenn Elementary. I had won the prize for being the best reader and writer in my whole grade. And now I was supposed to go back to an empty house and eat leftovers?

No way.

To cheer myself up, I headed over to the Short Stop to get a piece of pepperoni pizza. I was glad when I saw who was working behind the counter that evening. Gail talks a mile a minute and always knows the latest on everything, including me. As she rang me up, she asked about graduation and how it felt to be a big-shot seventh grader now. I had just finished showing off my trophy when I spotted a new ad tacked up on the bulletin board next to the checkout counter. I probably wouldn't have noticed it if it hadn't been written in cursive. No one writes in cursive any-more, especially in ads.

I wandered over with my pizza to take a closer look. "Want to get away from it all?" the sign said. "Rooms for rent at the former Fortune Consolidated School! BAR-GAIN RATES!—$25 a day / $35 with meals included." I studied the picture taped in the middle of the ad. I thought I knew every inch of Fortune, but somehow I'd never laid eyes on the school before. It looked like a man-sion, with its stone steps and three stories of dark-red brick. There was even a tower perched on the roof like a pointed crown. I scanned the flyer for an address, but somebody had already torn off the bottom piece that must have listed all the information.

"Hey, I've never seen this place before," I said to Gail. "How do you get there?"

"It's not too far off Front Street," she told me. "You take a right on Old Camp Road, go a little ways, and you can't miss it." She came over to gaze at the picture with a wist-ful smile. "My mother went to that school. And me and my brother too before they closed it down in the seventies when Fortune started running out of kids."

"It's crazy," she said over her shoulder as she stepped back to the cash register. "Hildy Baxter talked the county into selling her that old place for next to nothing a couple of months back, and now she's trying to fix it up and rent out rooms." Gail shook her head. "I don't know what she's thinking. She's way too old to be taking on that kind of a project. And Fortune isn't even a dot on the map anymore. Who in their right mind would want to live *there*?"

I would, I thought as I waved goodbye to Gail and went out front to eat my pizza at the picnic table. I'd climb up in that tower every day and invite all my friends to come over and explore.

I took my time at the Short Stop, chewing as slowly as possible and watching the rush of customers go by, dashing off to their weekend plans. But after my last bite, I still wasn't ready to go home. I decided to ride downtown to Mom's office and find out when she'd be done. I was used to her working late every so often, but she usually never stayed after hours on Fridays unless she was in the middle of tax season. Maybe she'd be finished earlier than she thought and I could talk her into taking me to get an ice-cream sundae at the Dairy Queen across the street.

Once I got to A-Plus Accounting, I left my bike in the alleyway next to Mom's building and headed to the back door since the front entrance is always locked after five. But something caught my attention as I rounded the corner to the parking lot. I stopped short in the alley. The lot was empty except for a black Jeep that sat idling next to Mom's car, and the Jeep's headlights were blinking on and off even though it wasn't dark outside.

Then I heard my mother's laugh. My throat tightened

with dread as I carefully peeked around the side of the building. Mom was standing on the back steps of her office. I watched in astonishment as she lifted her hand to wave at the person inside the Jeep.

I couldn't see the driver's face through the glare on the windshield, but I didn't need to. I knew exactly who drove that car, exactly who had a stupid plastic Hawaiian girl in a hula skirt mounted on his dashboard, ready to jiggle her hips whenever he put his foot on the accelerator. "Please! Call me Rick," he insisted to Nora and me the very first time we met. "*Mr. Littleton* makes me feel like an old geezer."

Mom had promised. She kept swearing she and Rick were just friends. Only a few days ago, I had confronted her again after she had joined Rick and his dog on one of their walks around the neighborhood. That's when Mom finally threw up her hands and said if it bothered me so much, she wouldn't hang out with him anymore. No more strolls to the park together. No more offering him iced tea on the front porch whenever he came over to fix something or mow our lawn. But there she was, smiling and clutching her purse to her side as she trotted over to his car in her wobbly heels and opened the passenger door.

"Your chariot awaits!" I heard Rick say.

Mom's high, breathless voice drifted toward me across the hot parking lot. "Where to?" she asked before she climbed inside. "I'm starving!"

My mouth filled with a bitter taste like metal as I hung back in the shadows, watching them drive away. *How could she?* How could she choose going to dinner with Rick instead of taking me out to celebrate my graduation? And what about Dad?

My father would be home from Afghanistan in thirty-six days. I had to do something. Something drastic.

The words from the ad at the Short Stop flashed through my head—*Want to get away from it all?*—and suddenly, I knew. I was going to Fortune and I wasn't coming home until Rick was out of our lives for good.

TWO

NO ONE WAS ANSWERING THE DOOR at the Fortune Consolidated School. There weren't any windows nearby to peek through, but I could hear the ugly blast of the buzzer echoing through the halls on the other side of the tall front doors. It sounded loud enough to wake the dead. Why wasn't anyone coming? Gail had said the landlady was really old. Maybe she was going deaf too.

I glanced over my shoulder at the sky settling into sweeps of purple and pink behind me. It would be dark soon. Still, I'd have climbed back on my bike and pedaled home if my tire hadn't started to go flat. The last stretch along the lonely country road, where the trees petered out and the cornfields began, had felt like I was pedaling through quicksand.

As soon as I rounded the bend on Old Camp Road and saw the school with its tower rising up over the fields like a deserted island, I realized I might have made a big mistake. The photo on the bulletin board at the Short Stop hadn't shown the peeling paint around the windows or the crumbling stone steps or the rusted parts of a forgotten playground poking up from the high grass nearby. If it hadn't been for a couple of cars in the parking lot and a room-rate sign taped on the front door, I would have thought the place was completely abandoned.

I hoisted my backpack higher on my shoulders and pressed the buzzer one last time. *This is it,* I told myself as I held the button down for three long seconds. *1001. 1002. 1003. If no one answers, I'll leave my bike in the ditch and walk home.* Maybe I'd even hitchhike. It would serve Mom right for refusing to let me have a cell phone until I started seventh grade. I was so ready to give up that I flinched in surprise when I heard the sharp click of a lock turning and someone grumbling on the other side of the doors.

"What do they think this is?" an old woman's voice croaked. "The Plaza Hotel?"

I flinched again when the door finally swung open and a blinding light shone in my face. I shielded my eyes. Was *that* Hildy Baxter? Listening to Gail, I had been imagining a plump grandmotherly sort of lady with white hair and spectacles. But the person at the door, with her face half hidden in the shadows of her flashlight, reminded me of one of those clowns you see in horror movies. She had on a lopsided brown wig and thick red lipstick smeared into her wrinkles, and she was wearing a droopy cardigan that hung like a sack on her stick-figure body.

"What on earth?" she said. Her voice was as rough as sandpaper.

"I'm looking for Mrs. Baxter?"

"That's me," she said. "I go by Hildy. What's this all about?"

My words came out in a rush. "I saw your ad at the Short Stop. My name's Ren Winningham, and I rode my bike here from Bellefield. I was wondering if I could rent one of your rooms."

She turned off her flashlight and reached over to flip a switch near the doorway. A fancy light fixture, piled with dead bugs, flickered on above her head. "Come in here where I can see you," she said.

I shuffled inside and stood blinking into the dim corners while Hildy lifted her eyeglasses from a chain around her neck, rammed them in place, and finished looking me over from head to toe. I tried to keep my nose from wrinkling. The school smelled like the terrarium I had made for my science project last year. Mossy and damp.

"How old are you?" she asked.

I swallowed hard so my voice would be steady. "Fourteen," I lied.

Her eyes narrowed behind her thick lenses. She tucked her flashlight in the pocket of her sweater and put her fists on her hips. "So you've run away from home."

"Oh, no," I said. "I just need a place to stay until . . ." My voice trailed off for a second. Why hadn't I practiced this part on my way over? "Until my mom and I get some things sorted out." I wriggled out of my backpack and dropped it on the floor like a bag of boulders. I should have felt better after that, but when I looked up at Hildy again, I felt my eyes start to sting and I had to suck in my breath so I wouldn't cry.

"Well, honey," she said. "I'm sorry, but the fact of the matter is I can't let you stay. You're underage."

Something about the way she called me honey suddenly made me want to keep trying. "But I can't go home now," I said, flapping my arms at my sides. "It's almost dark and my tire's flat."

Hildy peered around my shoulder at my bike parked out in the weeds and she blew out a heavy sigh. "How about if we call your mother and check this out with her? You got a phone?"

I shook my head no.

Her wig inched back and forth as she scratched the

stiff curls at the nape of her neck. I was bracing myself to be turned away when she pushed the front door closed and bolted the lock. *Was she really going to let me stay?*

She patted at the pockets of her sweater. "I must have left my phone back on the stage," she said with another ragged sigh. "Wait here while I go get it."

My heart sank. *Her phone?* Once she had disappeared down the murky hall, I anxiously checked my watch. It was after eight. Nora would be home from the diner by now and she'd have seen the note I had left for Mom on the kitchen counter. "I saw you with him tonight," I had written. "I've gone to Allison's and I'm not coming home until you get rid of him for good."

I paced back and forth under the small circle of light with my mind racing. This was crazy, but Mom had forced me into it. I couldn't remember my mother ever telling me a lie before—not even a white one. But after what I saw in the parking lot at her office, there was no denying it. *She had lied.*

I forced myself to take a few deep breaths. Nora would cover for me. Of course she would. She'd been just as worried as I had been about what was going to happen with Mom and Dad. She was even the one to come up with our private code: *Rick Alert.*

Before Dad had moved out, Mom had started picking on him about *everything.* How would he ever get promoted to manager at the printing plant now that he was leaving for a year? Why hadn't he gotten out of the army reserves when he had the chance? Why did he insist on keeping a smelly old hunting dog even though he barely went hunting anymore?

But whenever Rick was around, Mom turned into someone completely different. She acted like Allison did whenever she had a crush on a guy—all flirty and weird, asking him a flutter of questions about the bank he managed and what it was like volunteering for the Bellefield Rescue Squad. Nora started to take more notice after she found her missing Desert Bronze eye shadow in Mom's bathroom. *"Rick Alert,"* she had whispered when she showed me the evidence. We had never seen our mother wear eye shadow a single day in her life, and suddenly she was coming home from the drugstore with a tube of Big & Bold mascara and three colors of Covergirl Eye Enhancers.

In a few minutes Hildy was back, holding out a clunky flip-phone and fixing me with a no-nonsense stare. "The cell service out here is pretty hit or miss," she said as I reluctantly took the phone. "But I can usually get a signal when I'm in the foyer. Go ahead and give it a try." I edged away a few steps, nervously punching in my sister's number. I'd had it memorized ever since Nora had gotten her own phone when it was her turn to start junior high.

The call not only went through, but Nora picked up on the very first ring.

"Hi, Mom," I blurted out. I cleared my throat, fighting to keep from sounding so phony. "Yes, I'm totally fine. I'm sorry I ran out of the house like that. But I was so mad, I just needed to get away for a little while and think about things. And I figured you probably needed some space too, considering how much we've been fighting lately."

I closed my eyes as I pretended to be listening to my mother vent. I could hear Nora breathing on the other end, trying to absorb the situation. She finally spoke up in a strangled whisper. "What's going on?"

"I'm in Fortune," I babbled back at Nora. "At a rooming house."

"*What?* Your note said you're at Allison's," she hissed. "And what do you mean you're at a rooming house? There's no rooming house in Fortune. There's *nothing* in Fortune."

"Yes, there is," I said. "And Mrs. Baxter, she's the lady who owns this place, she says I can stay here if I have your permission." I glanced over my shoulder to flash a grateful smile at Hildy.

"Ren," Nora said. "What are you talking about? This is sounding really weird."

My pulse sped up. Hildy was motioning for me to hand over the phone. "Uh—here's the thing, Mom," I stammered. "Mrs. Baxter wants to talk to you and make sure it's all right for me to spend the night. You don't have to worry about the money part. I'm paying for everything myself. With my babysitting money. Okay? Here's Mrs. Baxter."

Please, Nora, I prayed as I thrust the phone at Hildy. I knew she could do it, as long as she didn't panic. My sister was good at acting. She had gotten a standing ovation at the high school last year when she played the part of the mother in *The Glass Menagerie.*

"Hello, this is Hildy Baxter," Hildy barked into the phone. "Yes, your daughter's fine. She seems like a real sweet girl. Sounds like you two just need a little time to cool off. She'll be perfectly safe here . . . if that's what you decide to do."

There was a long pause and then an uncomfortable, puzzled expression flickered over Hildy's face. I could hear the faint tinkle of Nora's voice chattering on and on at the other end. *Stop, Nora.* I pressed my knuckles against my mouth. *You're overdoing it.*

Hildy was shifting her feet restlessly. "No need for explanations, Ms. Winningham," she said. "I believe in giving people their breathing room. And if it makes you feel any better, I'm a mother too. I understand."

Hildy nodded. "You better write down my phone number though. Oh, you've already got it . . . Yes, that's all right with me. But you'll have to come and get her tomorrow, I suppose, because her bike tire's flat. When should we expect you? No . . . no, you don't need to give me an exact time. The afternoon works. We'll be here. See you then." My body tingled with relief as Hildy passed me back the phone.

I turned away. "See, Mom? She's really nice. And this is just what we need. A little time apart to . . . to take care of our *problem*," I added, exaggerating the last two syllables.

"Wait, *Ren*—" Nora almost screeched. "What's that lady going to think when Mom doesn't show tomorrow? And how long do you expect me to keep this up? Once Mom finds out you're not at Allison's, she's probably going to call the police."

I drifted away from Hildy again, holding my fingers over the tiny speaker on her phone. "Oh, that won't happen," I said. "You won't let it, right? Okay, Mom. Sounds good," I jabbered before she could squeeze in a reply. "Love you. Bye!" Then I punched my finger down on the red End button. I didn't have a plan for tomorrow afternoon, but suddenly I was too tired to care. I'd have to figure the rest out later.

I handed the phone back to Hildy and she grunted as she flipped it closed. "So I guess that's settled," she said, shaking her head. "That mother of yours sounds like a piece of work. I wasn't expecting her to let you stay . . . but at least she knows you're alive and kicking now. Come on. I'll show you to your room."

Once I had hefted up my backpack, Hildy switched off the overhead fixture and snapped on her flashlight again. "Watch your step," she told me. "I keep the lights off when I can. Otherwise I'd go broke paying the electric bills on this place."

THREE

A WAVE OF SHIVERS PRICKLED along the back of my neck as I followed Hildy through the entrance hall, watching the beam of her flashlight slide across the walls and past the dark corridors. Everywhere the light landed there seemed to be some creepy reminder of the past—rows of coat hooks and lockers, a rusted water fountain, and a glass display case that still had dusty trophies left inside. As Hildy led me up a wide staircase, I hung back on the landing, gripping the banister. The school felt haunted. I could have sworn I heard shuffling noises behind me and then a strain of faint piano music coming from somewhere above, but when I stole a look over my shoulder and cocked my head to listen, the sounds went quiet. I raced to catch up with Hildy. She was already rounding the corner at the top of the stairs.

"How many other people live here?" I asked as I tagged along on the second floor, eyeing the doors on either side of the hallway. Most of them stood open, revealing empty, shadowy rooms, but I could see a crack of light shining beneath one door halfway down the hall.

"Only six right now," Hildy told me. "But I'm hoping for more."

I thought of the "Welcome to Fortune" sign that I passed on my bike rides. Population: 12. So more than half of Fortune's residents lived right here in the school.

There was a big piece of plywood propped against the wall near the end of the corridor. Hildy stopped at the doorway just beyond it. "Room 26," she announced as she stepped through the entry and flipped on the overhead lights. "Nothing fancy, but the girls' washroom is right around the corner."

It was an old classroom with bare wooden floors—practically empty except for a metal chair and three cots lined up along the opposite wall. Each cot had a folded blanket and flat-looking pillow stacked at one end—sort of like the pictures Dad had sent of his army barracks in the desert.

"I forgot to ask if you're hungry," Hildy said. "Dinner's over, but if you come downstairs, Madeline can get you something to eat. She's not much of a cook." Hildy pressed her wrinkly red lips together. "But oh well, none of us have managed to starve to death so far."

"That's okay," I said. "I already ate, and I brought plenty of food." I gave my backpack a little pat. "Sandwiches and fruit . . . All kinds of stuff." Without knowing exactly how long I'd be staying, I didn't want to blow any of my precious babysitting money on meals.

"You sure?" Hildy's eyebrows drew together, making a sharp M across her forehead. It looked like she had drawn them on with a black Sharpie marker.

I nodded.

"Well, suit yourself," she said, turning to go. "I'll be back in a while to check on you."

"Sounds good. Thanks," I murmured as Hildy clicked on her flashlight again and shuffled off. I lowered my backpack and gazed toward the long row of windows and the blackness swallowing the sky beyond them. If only I had a phone. I could call Nora back and pour out everything that had happened that day in one long weepy gush. "Jeez, Ren," I could hear her saying. "You've really done it this time."

I turned away from the windows and straightened my shoulders. Staying in this place, even if it *was* haunted, would be a small price to pay for making Mom come to her senses.

At least that's what I told myself before I heard the crash right outside my door.

When I ran to the doorway and peered out, there was a little boy huddled on the floor next to the wall. He was staring at the long sheet of plywood that had been propped near the door. Now it was splayed flat on the ground beside him. The boy slowly turned to look up at me. In the shaft of light from the classroom, his eyes were as round and shiny as quarters.

"Shik," he said.

"Excuse me?"

"Mine says I can say that word if I change the last letter."

I might have laughed if my heart hadn't been lodged in my throat. "What happened?"

The boy turned to study the board again as if he was seeing it for the first time. "I guess I tripped," he said. He pushed himself to his feet and dusted off his skinny knees. He was wearing cargo shorts and Chicago Cubs bedroom slippers.

"So you live here?" I tried again.

"Yep. In the library." He crossed his arms. "I'm Hugh Miliken."

"Hi," I said stiffly. "I'm Ren."

"Like the bird."

"Oh, not that kind of wren. It's spelled R-E-N, not W-R-E-N. It's short for Renata."

"Oh. That makes more sense. You don't look anything like a bird."

I could see him sizing me up—my soccer-team T-shirt, my crazy hair. Most of it had exploded out of my ponytail during the bike ride. "You've sure got a lot of freckles," he said.

"Yep." What else was I supposed to say?

His eyes stayed riveted on my face. "Sometimes when I see people with freckles, I wish I could get a Magic Marker and connect the dots so I could see what picture comes out."

"Huh. Interesting." I smiled for the first time in hours. He was such a weird kid, I couldn't help it.

"Are you sure you're fourteen?"

I stopped and squinted down at him. "How'd you—?" I glanced at the board on the floor, putting two and two together. "Wait a minute. You were spying on us, weren't you? Downstairs. And out here in the hall . . ."

Instead of answering, Hugh looked down at his puny wrist and let out a gasp, which would have made sense if he had been wearing a watch, but he wasn't. "Oh, man, I better go," he said. "Mine's probably looking for me."

"Who's Mine?"

"That's my mom."

"So why do you call her Mine instead of Mom?"

Hugh's shoulders twitched with impatience. "It's a long story," he said. But then he told me the whole thing anyway. "We used to live in Chicago, and when I was really little, we would go to the park and the other kids would come up to my mom in the sandbox or on the swings and try to tell her stuff, and I would say, 'Mine! Mine!' because I didn't want to share her with anybody. Plus her real name is Madeline," he rattled on, "so now everybody, besides Hildy, copies me because Mine's way easier to say and takes up less time because it only has one syllable instead of three."

"Makes sense," I said.

"Hey," he said suddenly. "You know those cabinets in your room?"

I took a step back so that I could see past the threshold. Sure enough, there was a long row of cupboards running along the side wall. "Yeah?"

"I wouldn't open them if I were you." He hesitated. "Or actually, you can open all of them except the last one—the one on the end."

"What do you mean? Why shouldn't I open the one on the end?"

"You might sleep better tonight if you don't."

I started to ask what in the heck he was talking about. But all at once, he was checking his fake watch again. "Oops, time's up," he said. "Sayonara." Then he left me with my mouth still hanging open as I watched him scamper out of sight.

I turned toward the classroom again and stood frozen in the doorway, staring at the row of cabinets underneath the worn green countertop across the room. The last cabinet in the row looked like all the others—wooden with a small metal knob. My stomach flipped over at the thought of reaching out to open it. But how was I supposed to stay there if I didn't find out what was inside?

I marched over to the mystery cabinet. Then, holding my breath, I leaned down and snatched at the handle, scrambling backward as the door banged open. It was so dark inside the cupboard I could barely see. I crouched like a crab, bracing myself for who knows what to come popping out from the farthest corner.

But it was empty except for some dead bugs and cobwebs. I stood up and pivoted with my fists on my hips, warily eyeing the doorway. That little kid was probably still out there in the hall spying to see if I had fallen for his trick. Just to be sure though, I opened all the cabinet doors to take a quick peek inside. Empty . . . empty . . . empty . . . and then I let out a muffled shriek of surprise.

Somebody was staring back at me . . . or some *thing*. A grinning, hollow-eyed skull.

I shrank away and stayed stooped over for a few seconds, hugging myself, peering into the skull's empty sockets. Now I understood what that kid had been trying to tell me—to stay away from the cupboard on *this* end of the row, not the other. But how creepy could you get? What kind of people kept skulls in their cabinets and then left them there to freak out unsuspecting guests? I edged a little closer. I could see some other mysterious shapes sitting farther back in the shadows. I knelt down and leaned forward, straining to get a better view, but no matter what angle I tried, I couldn't quite see. "Ewww . . . ewww . . . *ewww*," I whined as I slowly reached my hand into the cabinet, past the skull's jutting jawbone and those bared yellow teeth. I grabbed at the largest object and pulled it toward me, sighing with relief as it came into the light.

It was one of those old-timey hourglasses—the same kind that the Wicked Witch in *The Wizard of Oz* uses to count down Dorothy's last hours. Kind of eerie, I thought as I turned the dusty wooden frame upside down and watched the sand trickle through the glass . . . but not nearly as creepy as the skull. I set the hourglass back in the cabinet and gritted my teeth as I groped for what looked like a small pile of shells. I snatched one from the pile and sat back on my heels to examine it. It had button holes punched through it, just like the shells I had seen heaped in the alleyways of Fortune.

None of it fit together. What did a skull have to do with an hourglass and a pile of used button shells?

I put the shell back and closed the cabinet, and while I was at it, I decided to close the classroom door too, thinking I might feel safer once I shut out the darkness on the other side. Then I grabbed my backpack and hurried over to sit on the middle cot. That's when I noticed there was a blackboard on the wall across from me with something written on it—a single word, dead center, scrawled in chalk.

NO

What did *that* mean? Was this supposed to be another prank like the skull, something to scare the roomers who were moving in? I knew it was crazy, but I couldn't help thinking the *no* was some sort of mysterious message meant only for me.

No, Ren, you shouldn't be here. Go back home where you belong.

My mouth had gone as dry as cotton balls, and all of a sudden I could hear every little sound—my breath turning shallow and the moths outside batting against the screens. There was nowhere to look without getting spooked. Not at the chalkboard or the cabinets or the row of pitch-black windows . . . I scooted my back against the wall and sat hugging my knees, fighting to stay calm. Part of me wanted to go find Hildy. But how could I trust the sort of landlady who kept a skull in her cupboard? And what would I say to Hildy once I found her? That I wanted to go home? Mom probably hadn't even been there to read my note yet. If I gave up now, my entire plan to get rid of Rick would fizzle out.

I unzipped my backpack and dumped everything on

the blanket. In my rush to leave the house I had thrown in all sorts of stuff—a toothbrush, three apples, my tattered copy of *Little Women*, two changes of underwear, three peanut butter sandwiches, some granola bars, a couple of T-shirts, a bottle of water, my zebra-stripe wallet, and my favorite picture of Dad, on the couch hugging Old Blue. Dad had sneaked him indoors one Sunday when it had snowed and Mom was off running errands. Nora had snapped the picture, saying she could use it for blackmail someday. We were in heaven that afternoon, Dad and Blue and me, tucked under the blanket watching the football game.

I stared at the photo for a while longer, letting the tears slide down and drip off my chin. Poor Dad. Poor Blue, stuck in that grubby dog pen in Uncle Spence's backyard.

When I finally raised my head, the word on the blackboard was shimmering in front of me.

NO

No, Ren, you can't give up.

I propped the picture on the chair beside my cot and carefully returned everything but the book to my pack, making sure to leave the squished sandwiches on top this time. Then I pulled off my shoes, lay back on the pillow, and settled in. At least I had *Little Women* to keep me company. I knew it was weird. Allison and Kelly never would have wanted to read a book that was written in 1868 and said corny things like "The four young faces on which the firelight shone brightened at the cheerful words . . ." I turned to chapter 22—my favorite—so I could read about how Marmee and the March girls have the best Christmas ever when Father surprises them and returns home from the Civil War.

FOUR

I SHOT UP IN THE COT, breathing hard. The classroom was bleached with sun. It took me a minute to take it all in—*Little Women* placed neatly beside Dad's picture on the chair, the blanket spread over my feet. Hildy must have come back to check on me and turn off the lights after I had fallen asleep. I swiped my hair out of my face and looked at my watch, still in a haze of disbelief. How could I have done it? Slept straight through till eight in the morning with all my worries about Mom and Rick, not to mention a skull lurking only a few feet away?

I had shoved my feet into my sneakers and was fumbling with the laces when I heard a sharp rap on the door. Hildy swept into the room before I had time to answer. She looked a lot less scary in the daytime, probably because her wig was on straight this morning and she had switched to pink lipstick instead of bloodred. She was wearing an old velour tracksuit that reminded me of dirty peach fuzz, but it was still a big improvement over yesterday's saggy sweater.

"Good. You're alive," she said. "You had me wondering last night. When I came back to see how you were doing, the light was on, but you were out cold. Must have been exhausted."

"Sorry about that," I said. "I can't believe I never woke up, especially after being so scared . . ."

"Scared?" Hildy's penciled-on eyebrows flew up. "Scared of what, for Pete's sake?"

There was no use beating around the bush. I went straight to the cabinet and flung the door open. *"That,"* I said, and scooted out of the way so she could see.

Hildy stepped closer, lifting her glasses from the chain around her neck and perching them on the end of her nose. She slowly leaned down to take a look. "Oh, lordy," she breathed. "You poor thing. I forgot all about Bonny's skull." She straightened up with a dry little chuckle.

"Bonny?"

"Mr. Bonnycastle. He taught here way back when I was in school. Reading and composition mainly, but once in a while he would hold an art class for the seniors. He was a fine artist himself. I remember he nabbed that skull from cranky old Mr. Prescott, who taught the sciences.

Then he set it up with the hourglass and the shells so he could teach us about drawing still-life pictures."

Hildy let her gaze roam wistfully around the room, then shook her head. "I should have pitched those things when I was clearing out this room a couple of months ago. But they brought back so many memories I couldn't stand to throw them away."

"So that's another thing I was wondering about," I said in a rush. I pointed at the mysterious word planted in the middle of the chalkboard. "What does *that* mean?"

Hildy blinked. "Oh, that?" She frowned and fidgeted with the zipper of her jacket. "That was Garrett's bright idea. He's my handyman. He's been checking all the rooms for any last repairs that need to be done. If there aren't any, he writes *no* on the board and moves on."

I felt the knot in my throat loosen. Her explanations sounded so reasonable.

"I should be getting downstairs," Hildy said. She pushed up her sleeves. "I got a big surprise this morning. My son called at the crack of dawn to say he's driving over from Des Moines today. He's bringing my grandson Tucker with him."

I waited for Hildy to smile. "Aren't you glad they're coming?" I asked.

"Sure, I am. It'll be good to see them, especially Tucker. I bet he's grown a foot. But to tell the truth," she said, "my son, Jack, didn't exactly like the idea of me investing in this place. He hasn't bothered to visit or help out since I moved here. And now, all of a sudden, he's got a bee in his bonnet and claims he wants to see how I'm doing." Hildy's voice sounded like a rubber band ready to snap. "Anyway"—she waved her hand like she was shooing flies—"he says they'll be staying for dinner, so I need to let Madeline know." She bobbed her head toward the door. "Why don't you come with me and get some breakfast?"

"Oh, no thanks." I reached up to scrape my tangled hair back into its ponytail. "I brought my own food, remember?"

"Baloney," Hildy said. "I'm not about to let a young girl starve on my watch. Let's go. We can stop by the washroom on our way down."

I hurried over to dig my wallet out of my backpack so I could at least pay Hildy what I owed for the room so far. She lit up like she had won the lottery when I pressed my crumpled bills into her hand.

FIVE

THIS TIME I KNEW the piano music wasn't my imagination. There was a slow, waltzy sort of tune drifting from somewhere close by. Before I could ask Hildy where it was coming from, she sped up in front of me. "There he is again!" she cried. "How many times do I have to tell those silly women?" I had no idea what she was talking about until I noticed a cat pawing furiously at one of the closed doors halfway down the hall—the same door where I had seen the sliver of light the night before.

Hildy moved surprisingly fast for an old lady. As she barreled closer, the cat sank into a crouch, poised to scamper away. For a second, I thought Hildy intended to snatch him up by the scruff of his neck. But when she reached him, she only shooed him aside with her foot and knocked sharply on the door where he'd been pawing.

The waltz stopped and the cat sat back on his haunches. I had never seen an animal like that before—tawny gold with black stripes on his legs and black spots on his back. He looked like he had stepped straight out of the jungle, except he was small like a house cat and tame.

The door cracked open, just enough to see part of a woman's face peering out. "Colette, one of these leopard cats of yours is out here again," Hildy snapped.

"Oh, naughty Flam," the woman scolded. "Where have you been?" Her voice was strangely hushed, the way people talk when they're in church or a museum. "Just a minute," she said through the crack. "Clarissa's catching Flim before he runs off too."

The door finally swung open a little wider and a second woman appeared behind the first one, holding another cat. I felt like I was seeing double. The cats were identical and the ladies looked like twins—the same plain wide faces, the same straight mouse-brown hair cropped at their chins. They smiled in unison as they watched their missing cat dart back inside.

But as soon as the second woman spoke, I could tell the sisters were completely different. "We've told you, Hildy," she barked. "Flim and Flam aren't leopards. They're Bengal house cats and I don't know why you're so upset. We should let them get loose more often. They could probably help a lot with all the mice around this place."

"You know my rules, Clarissa," Hildy told her. "You can take them or leave them."

Neither of the sisters had noticed me waiting out in the hall. And Hildy seemed to have forgotten I was there as she continued to argue with Clarissa about the best pet policy for the school. But from where I was standing, I could see a sliver of the room behind them—an old piano in front of a sunny window and a cat-climbing structure covered in bright green shag. And there was a wonderful flowery smell like rose petals wafting through the doorway.

"We'll try to do a better job of keeping an eye on them," Colette soothed in her feathery voice. "Won't we, Clarissa?" Clarissa gave a begrudging nod.

Hildy thanked the sisters before Colette closed the door, but she was still grumbling as I followed her down the stairs. "They never told me they were bringing those darn cats," she fussed. "I let them have the music room. I let them bring in a man to tune the piano, and I even let them haul a stove up there so they could make that highfalutin soap of theirs." She paused on the landing to catch her breath. "The least they can do is keep those animals from prowling around, jumping out and scaring me half to death."

Hildy must have noticed I wasn't listening anymore. She followed my gaze up to the wall above the landing.

"Isn't that a pretty mural?" she said. "That's what the riverfront in Fortune looked like once upon a time."

Dusty rays of sunshine streamed through the high window over the stairwell, lighting up a large wall painting of girls in aprons and boys in overalls gathered on the banks of the Mississippi. The view was from the water with the school set off in the distance, reigning over the scene from its rise of land. I tilted my head, trying to make sense of the other details. There were two boats heading toward the shore, and the children held buckets. One had what looked like a rake in his hand.

"What are those kids doing?" I asked.

"Clamming," Hildy said. "When my older brother, Tom, was a boy, he could go down to that spot on the river and scoop up mussels and clams by the bushelful. In those days most of the families around here were involved with button-making in one way or another, and the kids would help out whenever they could. My father had a clamming boat and Tom spent all his summers working on it. He had big dreams of running his own button factory some day."

"Did he do it?" I asked. "Open a button factory?"

Her watery eyes dimmed. "No, he didn't get the chance. The button business went bust and then he was one of the first soldiers to be called up for the Korean War. Poor Tom never came home."

"I'm sorry," I said quietly. "My father's in Afghanistan right now. He's been there for almost a year."

"Good heavens." Hildy winced. "That must have been his picture I saw last night next to your cot."

I nodded, and she patted my arm. "Don't you worry, honey. That mess in the Middle East is nothing like the war my brother was in. Your father's going to be just fine."

I followed Hildy to the bottom of the stairs. The foyer still looked lonely in the daylight, but not nearly as gloomy as the night before. Someone had brought my bike inside and propped it next to a kid's scooter near a door with a frosted glass window marked SCHOOL OFFICE. The trophy case stretched across the other end of the foyer under a banner that I hadn't noticed last night. HOME OF THE FORTUNE HUNTERS, it proclaimed in faded green letters trimmed with gold. The words drifted through my head as Hildy led me along one of the wings off the foyer. *Fortune Hunters.* It sounded so glamorous compared to the Bellefield Bulldogs.

Hildy stopped and rapped on another door with a frosted window. This one said LIBRARY—QUIET PLEASE, but when we entered the rambling space where Hugh and his mother lived, I felt like I was stepping into a genie's den. The wooden floors were covered with a patchwork of worn Oriental carpets, oversize cushions, and beanbag chairs. Even the ceiling, draped in lengths of gauzy fabric, looked exotic. The only traces of a library I could see were a tattered set of encyclopedias lining the windowsill and one of those giant card catalog cabinets filled with row after row of little drawers. Dad had shown me a card catalog in an antiques store once. "Whoa, that's crazy," I remember saying when he had explained how people used to find books in libraries before computers came along and took over all the dirty work.

"Yoo-hoo!" Hildy called. "Anyone home?"

A wisp of white-blond hair and half of a face appeared around the corner of the card catalog. "Oh, there you are, Hugh," Hildy said. "Come on out here. I'd like to introduce you to someone. This is Ren."

Before I could open my mouth to say we had already met, Hugh was zigzagging toward me, dodging around the floor cushions. He dumped the heavy book he had been carrying on a nearby beanbag chair and tucked a yellow pencil behind his ear. "Nice to meet you," he said, thrusting out his hand.

I hesitated, then took Hugh's hand and gave it a clumsy shake. "Hi there," I answered. Why was he pretending he had never seen me before? As soon as I let go of his hand, Hugh hoisted up his book again. *Birds of North America*, it was called, and an index card covered in kidlike writing stuck out from the pages.

"So where'd your mother get off to?" Hildy asked.

"She's in the kitchen trying to make muffins."

"What do you mean *trying*?" a voice said behind us. A woman came in from the hallway with the tail of her filmy skirt swishing along the floor. I tried not to stare. I had never met anyone with dreadlocks before. Hers were strawberry blond and her nose was pierced with a diamond that sparkled like a teeny tiny raindrop. "I made two dozen," she said proudly, drying her hands on a red bandanna. "And they're bran, so they're extra healthy."

"Madeline, this is Ren," Hildy said. "I'm sure she'd be happy to give those muffins of yours a try. She hasn't had breakfast yet."

"Great." Hugh's mother studied me with a tired smile. She wiped her flushed face with the bandanna and then used it to tie her dreads into a ponytail. "You can call me Mine, by the way." I nodded. "How long will you be staying?" she asked.

Hildy answered for me. "Her mother's picking her up this afternoon. But we'll need to set two extra places for dinner tonight. My son and his youngest boy, Tucker, are coming for a visit. They'll be here sometime after lunch."

"Really?" Mine's gray eyes widened in alarm.

"Really. So I thought I better warn you. That tofu dish we had last night isn't the kind of thing that'll go over very well with my son. He's more the meat-and-potatoes type."

Mine sniffed. "That's fine, but I guess I'll need to make a trip into Bellefield. We're running a little low on *meat*

45

at the moment." Her lips curled around the word with distaste. "And sorry, Hildy, but I'm almost out of the grocery money you gave me last week."

Hildy winked at me as she reached into the pocket of her tracksuit and handed Mine the money I had paid her. But then her expression darkened as she caught sight of the old clock that hung over the library windows. "Holy smokes! I need to get moving. They'll be here before we know it."

I could feel Mine watching me as Hildy hurried off. I knew she must be wondering where I came from and why I was there, but she didn't ask me any questions. "I can show you where to get breakfast on my way out," she said as she walked over to unhook her crocheted satchel from the coat tree in the corner. "Hey, mister," she called to Hugh, "we better get going too if we want to be ready for the carnivores."

Hugh didn't answer. He was poking along the front of the card catalog, holding the index card from the bird book and studying the labels on the alphabetized wooden drawers. "R . . . R . . ." I heard him whisper to himself. "R for Ren, not W."

I watched as Hugh stopped halfway down the card catalog, stood on his tiptoes, and opened the R drawer. From where I was standing, it looked like all the original cards listing the library books had been removed. Without even glancing inside, Hugh dropped his own card into the empty drawer and quietly slid it shut.

"Hey, buddy," Mine said, louder this time. "Up and at 'em. Time for grocery shopping."

Hugh whipped around, bursting out of his silence like a boiling teakettle. "Do I have to? Can't I stay here? With Ren?"

Mine looked baffled. "But you love going into town. And Ren . . . well, she doesn't even know us. And she might not want any company right now." She glanced over at me with an apologetic smile. "Right?"

"Oh, I don't mind," I said.

"Are you sure?" Mine asked, once Hugh had run off to put his bird book away. "You don't mind keeping an eye on him while I'm gone?"

"Not a bit," I told her. Sure, her son might be a little on the strange side. But I was almost certain he'd be better company than Mr. Bonnycastle's skull.

SIX

I WAS SO HUNGRY that anything would have tasted good—even Mine's muffins that made a thud when she dropped one on my plate before she headed off to the grocery store. Luckily she had also poured us glasses of milk to help wash things down. I sat with Hugh at a red Formica table in the kitchen in front of the old serving window, peering out at the giant room on the other side. It was empty except for two picnic tables with benches that had been pushed together end to end. The cafetorium, Hugh called it. "Because it's half cafeteria, half auditorium," he said. Then he pointed to the stage that stretched across the opposite side of the room. "Hildy lives up there."

I might not have believed him if I hadn't heard her bumping around behind the red velvet curtains, getting ready for her son's visit. The stage actually seemed like a pretty smart choice for a bedroom, considering how close it was to the kitchen. I glanced around. Nothing in the kitchen matched anymore. There was a gold fridge and an avocado-green stove, and long rows of cupboards painted the color of canaries. And the kitchen felt lots homier than a cafeteria, with its smell of coffee and molasses and the trail of mixing bowls and muffin tins that Mine had left spread across the metal counters.

Hugh gnawed a tiny chunk off the top of his muffin. "Tastes like birdseed," he said. Then his face spread into a grin, wide enough for me to see his big front teeth. "That must be why you like it. Because you're a wren. Did you know wrens are famous for their loud and complex songs?"

"No, I didn't," I said through my bite of muffin. "But that's probably exactly how my sister would describe me. Loud and complex." I took another swig of milk. "Is that what you were looking up in that bird book? Wrens?"

Hugh nodded. "I like to keep notes on people."

"So how come you didn't tell Hildy and your mom that we had already met last night? Was it because you didn't want them to know I caught you spying on me?"

"I don't know what you're talking about," Hugh said, but I could see a flush of red creeping up his pale neck.

When I raised one eyebrow at him, he turned away, rushing to change the subject. "I wish I could have Lucky Charms instead of this yucky muffin." He pointed to some cereal boxes that sat on top of the refrigerator.

"Why can't you?"

"Mine only lets me eat sugar cereal on my birthday. They'll probably be stale by then." He was quiet for a second, studying my expression. "I'm eight. But I bet you thought I was only seven, right?"

I shrugged. He was definitely smaller than the average eight-year-old, but he seemed wiser somehow with his silvery gray eyes and that pencil perched behind his ear. "I wasn't sure how old you were . . . just like you didn't know whether I was fourteen or not." I broke into a sly smile. "Come on, admit it. You were spying last night."

Hugh thumped his muffin down on his plate. "All right, all right, I was spying." He sighed. "I'm usually really good at it."

"So it sounds like this is something you do a lot—this spying thing."

"Yeah, but you're the first person who's caught me since we moved here," Hugh boasted. "Hildy's never caught me. And Mine, she knows that I wander off sometimes, but she doesn't know exactly what I'm up to."

"What *are* you up to?" I asked.

Hugh's face grew solemn. "There's a lot of strange stuff going on around this place. I'm trying to figure it out."

"Really? You mean like those weird things under the sink in my room?"

Hugh sat up straight. "So you saw the skull?" he asked gleefully. "Were you scared?"

"Petrified," I said. "Until Hildy came in this morning and explained about her teacher and the art lessons."

"Yeah. Mr. Bonnycastle. He sounds cool. I told Hildy she should put the skull in her museum, but she says it doesn't really fit with her theme."

"Museum? What museum?"

"It's in the gym. It's sort of hard to explain." Hugh hopped up from the table. "But I can show you if you want."

"Sure," I said. Then I glanced around the messy kitchen. "Right after we do these dishes."

Once we had finished, Hugh led me back through the foyer to the opposite end of the school. But even when I stood in the doorway of what used to be the gym, staring out at the so-called museum, I still didn't understand. All I could see was a ton of junk spread from one basketball hoop to the other. I gawked up at the narrow balcony that ran around the sides of the sprawling room. In the old days people probably lined up along the railings to look down and watch games, but now even the balcony was jammed with junk.

"What is all this stuff?" I whispered.

"It's going to be a pearl-button museum," Hugh said. He had already started down one of the cramped pathways that led through the piles, and I followed slowly along, examining the clutter on either side—rusted machinery with cranks and foot pedals, washtubs full of different kinds of shells, clamming rakes, and sawhorses stacked with old metal signs that said "American Maid Button Manufacturers" and "Style Right Buttons—Jewel of the Mississippi."

"Gosh, my dad would love it here," I said.

Hugh seemed surprised. "He would? Mine's worried. She says people go to museums to see dinosaurs or mummies or planetariums or IMAX movies. Like they've got in Chicago." He stopped next to a burlap bag full of discs that looked like miniature checkers. "She doesn't think people really care about buttons."

I scooped up a handful of the discs. They were white on one side and brown on the other. "Those are button blanks," Hugh said. He sounded like a tour guide. "That's what buttons used to look like before they polished off the outside part and drilled in the holes."

So these were the missing pieces—the circles that had been punched out of all those shells in the alleyways of Fortune and the little pile of shells in the cabinet upstairs. I rubbed my finger over the white side of one of the blanks in my palm. It was smooth and let off a little gleam of light like a pearl, which probably explained how the buttons got their name.

"You can keep one if you want," Hugh offered. "Hildy won't mind. She says she's going to give a button blank to every single person who visits her museum." He rooted in the side pocket of his cargo shorts. "Here's mine." He opened his fist to show me the one he'd been carrying. "It's my lucky charm."

"Way better than cereal," I joked. "Never goes stale."

Hugh smiled crookedly. "Hey, that's a good one. I gotta write that down." He reached for the pencil behind his ear and pulled a fresh index card out of his pocket. As Hugh wandered ahead scribbling, I hung back and sifted through a few more handfuls of button blanks, searching for one that struck my eye. I'd never had a good luck charm before and suddenly it seemed like something I desperately needed.

After I had chosen my favorite blank and tucked it in my pocket, it took me a while to find Hugh in the maze of cardboard boxes. "Ahoy!" he yelled when I came around a stack of storage bins. I laughed in amazement. He was standing inside a boat—a big one—that looked like it had run aground on the only island of empty space in the gym.

"This is the best part of the whole museum," Hugh declared. "It's a clamming boat. It used to be Hildy's dad's." The wooden boat sat about three feet off the ground on a makeshift platform. It was long and flat-bottomed and smelled like it had a fresh coat of paint—emerald green with bright white trim.

"Isn't it great?" Hugh asked me. "I just wish we could name it something different."

"Why, what's it called?"

Hugh didn't answer. He rolled his eyes, jerking his

thumb toward the back of the boat. I walked around to read the name that was painted across the stern in white capital letters. "What's wrong with *Little Miss*?" I asked. "I think it's cute. It's short for Mississippi, right?"

"That's the problem. A boat shouldn't sound *cute*. Why couldn't Hildy's dad have called it something like *Sea Witch*? Or *Discovery*. That's what Lewis and Clark named theirs. Those guys never would have gone exploring in a boat called *Little Miss*."

He had a point. The name sounded too sweet, especially considering the scary contraption full of long hooks that ran along the length of one side. "That's the clamming rig," Hugh told me, slipping into his tour guide routine again. He explained how the clammers used to drag all those hooks along the bottom of the river and the dopey mussels and clams got fooled into thinking the hooks were something tasty or an enemy floating by, so they chomped their two halves down on them. "And *whammo*," Hugh said, smacking his hands together. "After that, they got their insides boiled out and their outsides cut into buttons."

"Yuck." I grimaced.

Hugh swung his legs over the side of the boat and hopped from the platform to the floor. "Come on," he said. "I have to show you one more thing." I scrambled after him as he ducked under another set of sawhorses. I flinched when we popped up next to a pair of spooky mannequins with yellow hair like straw. They were wearing matching vests decorated in a gleaming assortment of buttons, but I couldn't stop to take a closer look. Hugh had already disappeared again. I squeezed past another row of old-fashioned machines, wrinkling my nose at the smell of engine grease. Hugh was on the other side holding a photograph in a silver frame.

"Guess who?" he said, handing me the picture. I stared at the pretty girl who waved from the black-and-white photograph. She wore a puffy white dress and a tall crown, and she sat on a throne tucked inside a giant fake clamshell. It looked like she was riding on a fancy float like the ones in the Macy's parade that Nora and I watched on TV every Thanksgiving.

"Is that—?"

"It's Hildy!" Hugh pointed to the words engraved on the bottom of the frame. *Queen of the Fortune Button Festival—June 1950.* "She says she was the last queen ever because the river ran out of shells and they stopped having the festival."

I bent closer. "She was so beautiful." The girl in the picture had a cloud of dark wavy hair and china-doll skin, but you could still tell it was Hildy, even without the wrinkles and lipstick and the lopsided wig. She had the same mischief in her smile, the same stubborn tilt to her chin.

"Look how happy they all are," I said as I stared at the faces in the crowd. "I'm glad Hildy's making a museum.

Otherwise how would people know this stuff ever happened?"

Hugh took the picture and set it back in its stand on a card table. "You want to see her crown?" he asked. "It's made out of buttons." He picked up a pink velvet bag from the corner of the table, but before he could get the drawstring untied, we heard Hildy's raspy voice. It sounded like she was coming down the hall, talking to somebody on her cell phone.

"Say that again," I heard her squawk. "We got a bad connection. I can't quite hear you." My heart jumped. What if she was talking to Mom? Had Nora given up and spilled the beans already?

Hugh held a finger to his lips and pulled me down to a crouch. Then he motioned for me to stay low and follow him through another obstacle course of cardboard boxes and wooden crates. When we finally stood up straight, we were in a dark storage room off the gym.

"What's going on?" I whispered. "Why are we hiding?"

"I don't want Hildy to see us," Hugh said softly. "She doesn't like me exploring the museum when she's not there." Before I could wonder more about who Hildy had been talking to or whether she was looking for me, Hugh grabbed my hand. The next thing I knew, we were stepping out into the blinding sunlight and a flower garden that bordered the side of the school.

On the other side of the garden there were two women in sun hats bent over a row of white flowers. They straightened in surprise when they spotted us. When one of them pushed back the brim of her hat, I realized who they were—the sisters from the second floor. I could tell they expected us to stop and say hello, but Hugh was already scurrying along a dirt path that led back to the front of the school. I gave the sisters a little half wave and trotted after him.

Hugh didn't slow down until he had rounded the corner of the building and slipped behind a gnarled lilac bush. "Jeez," I huffed once I had scooted into the space beside him. "What's going on? I feel like I'm in a video game dodging old ladies."

Hugh leaned his back against the brick wall of the school to catch his breath. "That was Sister Loud and Sister Soft," he panted, and readjusted the pencil behind his ear. "They're always trying to get me to help pull weeds in their soap garden. If we had stopped, I'd never get to finish showing you around."

I leaned against the wall beside him. The bricks felt warm on my back. "You really call them that?" I smiled. "Sister Loud and Sister Soft?"

"Not to their faces. Just with Mine. We can't tell them apart unless they're talking . . . or yelling." Hugh peeked out from the branches of the lilac to check whether the coast was clear. When he turned back to me, his expression was somber. "Are you afraid of heights?" he asked.

"Um. What kind of heights?"

Hugh pointed past the fading purple blooms over my head. I took a careful step out from under the bush and squinted into the sunlight. He was pointing at the tower.

SEVEN

TO GET TO THE TOWER, we had to go back inside, make our way to the third floor, open a narrow door hidden in a crook of the hall, and climb up twelve more steep steps. At the top, Hugh shoved open a trapdoor. I clambered through after him and stood up slowly, reaching for the railing to steady myself. When I looked out, my stomach flipped over and my breath caught in my throat. You could see forever—past the cornfields, past the roofs of Fortune poking up through the trees, all the way to the Mississippi River. Dad likes to call it the Mighty Mississippi, but the river didn't look so mighty from up in the tower. It looked more like a flat brown snake sliding across the countryside.

I could tell Hugh had been up in the tower before. He

didn't even bother to grab the railing as he stepped around the trapdoor and looked down on the backyard of the school. "Whoa," he said. "Garrett got a lot more shells this morning."

I edged over to see what he was talking about. I squeezed my eyes shut and opened them again, trying to make sense of the strange scene below. There was an old baseball diamond out back, and surrounding it were mountains and mountains of salt-and-pepper-colored shells. At the edge of the ring, a huge man with a scruffy blond beard stood in the back of a green pickup truck shoveling more shells on top of another pile. So that was Garrett, Hildy's handyman who wrote on the blackboards. Hugh had pointed out the door to his room on the third floor when we were on our way up to the tower.

"What the heck is he doing?" I asked.

"Making a labyrinth."

"A labyrinth?"

"It's kind of like a maze," Hugh explained. "Garrett used to fix up old castles and churches in England, where they had a lot of that kind of stuff. He says he's always wanted to make a labyrinth. And he thinks it'll help get more people to come see the museum."

"Wow," was all I could say. I had been in corn mazes before, and Nora and I had gotten lost in a giant boxwood maze when we went on vacation to Colonial Williamsburg. But I'd never heard of anything like that being made out of shells. Then again, I'd never heard of a button museum until about an hour ago.

While we were watching Garrett, I began noticing all the graffiti in the tower. It wasn't like the graffiti I had seen scribbled in bathroom stalls and under the bleachers at school. It was the antique kind—hundreds of names and sayings carved on the floor and the railing. There were so many, it seemed like every kid who had ever gone to school in Fortune must have owned a pocketknife and climbed up to leave a mark in the tower. *FCS is the Best!* . . . *Peggy Anne and Emma Jean—Friends 4Ever* . . . *Fortune Hunters-B.Ball Champs of '69.*

Hugh called me over to see a carving on the handrail.

HAZEL DOBBS
LOVES
WALTER NUTT

"If they got married," he said, barely able to contain himself, "her name would be Mrs. Hazel Nutt." He started laughing so hard, showing those funny front teeth of his, that I got the giggles too and couldn't stop until Hugh knelt down and pointed to where Hildy had carved her name on the floor near the trapdoor when she was a kid.

HILDA LARSON — CLASS OF '50

"How do you know that's her?" I asked.

"Because she asks me to get her mail out of the mailbox by the road sometimes, and I've seen that name on her letters. Hilda Larson Baxter."

"So she must have been picked to be the button queen right after she finished high school." I kept staring at the date on the floor, trying to add up the numbers in my head. "If Hildy was eighteen when she graduated," I said, "that means she's got to be . . . more than eighty years old."

"Whoa," Hugh said.

We were still on our knees talking about how peppy Hildy was for being so ancient when we heard a huge commotion below—a roaring engine and hissing brakes and some sort of weird high-pitched braying sound. Hugh scrambled to his feet. "Mayor Joy's back!" he cried.

I followed him to the front railing just in time to see a man hop down from the cab of a tractor-trailer truck in the parking lot. "Hey there, buddy," the truck driver called out. I couldn't tell who he was talking to. Then a donkey emerged from the high grass near the old playground, wheezing out a stream of hee-haws as he clopped across the gravel.

"That's Wayne," Hugh said.

"Which one?"

Hugh laughed. "The donkey. He hates it when the Mayor goes away on long hauls. Garrett takes good care of him, but Wayne likes Mayor Joy a lot better."

I sized up the man below. He was old too—not as old as Hildy, but his bald head shone like polished mahogany next to his snow-white sideburns. "Is that another one of your nicknames? Mayor Joy?"

Hugh shook his head. "No, he's really the mayor. And his last name is really Joy."

"What's he the mayor of?"

"Fortune."

"Fortune? But Fortune's not even a town anymore, is it? It only has twelve people."

Hugh shrugged. "Beats me. All I know is that's what people call him, and Hildy says he's been the mayor forever."

The Mayor's kindly voice drifted up to us as he stood rubbing Wayne between his oversize ears, carrying on like they were long-lost friends. I lifted my hand to wave.

"Don't!" Hugh said under his breath. He grabbed my arm, tugging me back from the railing.

"How come?"

"I don't want Mine to find out we were up here. She thinks it's too dangerous. And she says I'm allergic to wasps."

I stopped breathing for a second. "Wasps? What wasps?"

Hugh nodded up at the rafters. Two wasps were circling lazily over our heads. I felt my stomach go watery. I could see a giant wasp nest lodged between the roof supports of the tower. "Hugh," I gasped. "Why didn't you tell me you aren't allowed up here? Or in the museum? Your mom's going to think I'm the worst babysitter ever."

Hugh flinched like I had pinched him. *"Babysitter?"* he said. Then he spun away, sending his pencil flying. He marched for the trapdoor and lowered himself through.

"Wait, Hugh," I called as I floundered after him. It wasn't easy to wrestle the hatch closed and pick my way down the steep steps. I thought Hugh would be gone when I finally stumbled out to the third floor, but he was sitting at the top of the main staircase with his elbows on his knees and his chin propped in his hands. I plopped down next to him and held out his pencil. "Sorry if I hurt your feelings," I said. "I didn't mean that I think you're a baby or anything."

Hugh tucked his pencil behind his ear again and scowled down at his Cubs slippers. "I thought we were hanging out because you wanted to be friends," he said, "not because you thought you were supposed to be my *babysitter*." He spit out the word like it was a bad taste on his tongue.

"I *do* want to be friends," I said. "It's just that I don't want to break any rules while I'm here . . . I'm in enough trouble as it is."

Hugh finally looked up at me. "'Cause you ran away from home, right?"

I blinked at him in surprise. Then I remembered. Spymaster Hugh had heard everything that had happened in the foyer when I first arrived. "Yeah," I admitted softly.

"Mine and I sort of ran away from home too."

"Really? How come?"

"Mine said Chicago wasn't good for us anymore and we needed a fresh start."

The forlorn note in Hugh's voice tugged at my heart. No wonder he was so desperate for friends. It had to be lonely being the only kid wandering around this old school. Plus I hadn't seen a single TV or computer since I arrived. "If you want, I could ride my bike over and visit you sometimes," I offered. "Once I go home. I don't live very far away."

Hugh gave me a skeptical look. "Yeah, that's what Cal said too—that he'd come and visit, but he never did."

"Who's Cal?"

"He was Mine's boyfriend. He's been my favorite so far. He used to take me to see the Cubs, and he taught me how to play video games and say cuss words in Spanish. All sorts of stuff. But Mine thought he was a bad influence so they broke up."

"Sorry," I said. "That stinks."

"So what should we do now?" Hugh asked. "When do you think your mom'll be here?"

I shifted on the steps uneasily. "Oh, I don't know. This afternoon sometime." I glanced at my watch. I only had a few more hours to come up with an explanation, some way to convince Hildy that it would be okay for me to stay longer.

I pushed myself to my feet and meandered a little farther down the hall, peering into classrooms. Each one had a chalkboard with the word *no* written across the middle. When I stopped in the doorway of what looked like an old chemistry lab, Hugh appeared at my side and pushed his way past me. "Look," he said, opening a cabinet under one of the tall lab tables. The shelves inside were filled with beakers and bottles containing the remnants of mysterious-looking powders and liquids. "I'm going to borrow Hildy's rubber gloves sometime and Mine's sunglasses so I can mix these together and see what happens."

I was barely listening as he rattled on about the experiments he wanted to try. Another *no* was scrawled across the board at the front of the room, which didn't make sense considering there was a big black stain on the ceiling nearby and a cluster of buckets positioned underneath.

"That's a pretty bad leak," I said.

Hugh came to stand beside me. "Yeah, it happened during that giant storm we had last week. Garrett tried to fix it but he couldn't. He says we've got to call a roofer."

I pointed at the blackboard. "So why'd he write *no* on the board if this room still needs repairs?"

"What do you mean? Garrett didn't do that. Hildy did."

"But Hildy said Garrett's the one who writes on the boards."

Hugh pursed his lips together, then hurried over to peek out the doorway and check in both directions. He motioned me closer. "That's what I was telling you about—all the weird stuff going on around here. Hildy's been looking for something. She searches at night when she thinks everybody's asleep. And whenever she's done with one room and hasn't found anything, she writes *no* on the board and goes to the next one."

"What's she looking for?" I whispered.

"I'm not sure. But she started up on the third floor. By the time Mine and I moved in, she was almost finished up there and then she did the second floor. She finally got all the way down to the basement a few nights ago, and I think she must have found something because she hasn't been out looking ever since."

"Well?" I stared at him. "What was it?"

"I told you." Hugh bounced on his toes in frustration. "I don't know. It was really creepy and dark down there, with lots of corners so I could barely see." Then he stopped, peering at me. "But I know how we can figure it out. You want to help me?"

I crossed my arms, trying to imagine what I might be

getting myself into this time. "It depends. Does it involve anything dangerous? Like wasps or heights?"

"Nope." Hugh shook his head back and forth. "Nothing dangerous."

"Will we be breaking any rules?"

He squinted, considering. "I don't think so."

"That doesn't sound very convincing."

But before I could ask any more questions, Hugh was dashing down the hall. "Come on," he cried over his shoulder. "We've got to hurry before Mine gets back."

So much for staying out of trouble.

EIGHT

HUGH SLIPPED THROUGH THE DOOR of the principal's office first. I hung back in the main office a little longer, glancing at the spot behind the long wooden counter where the school secretary would have sat. The rows of mail cubbies covering the wall nearby were still labeled with the names of all the teachers in alphabetical order. Miss Atkinson . . . Mr. Barbour . . . A flurry of butterflies rose in my chest. According to Hugh, the principal's office wasn't off-limits. But for some reason he had wanted to make sure Hildy was occupied in another part of the school before we went inside. It only took us a few minutes to track her down. When we looked in the gym, we spotted her deep in conversation with the Mayor. So the coast was still clear, at least for a little while.

I checked over my shoulder one last time and stepped

through the doorway. Hugh was standing behind a massive metal desk in the middle of the stuffy room. A window faced out to the front of the school, but it was shut tight, with a sprinkle of dead flies scattered along the sill.

"Okay, let's have it," I said. I could almost taste the mildew rising up from the worn gold carpet. "What're we doing here?"

Hugh opened the top drawer of the desk. "I wanted to show you this."

I walked over to see what he was pointing at. "You wanted to show me a bunch of old thumbtacks?"

"No, *this*." He pushed the tacks and paper clips aside and tapped his finger on a small square of paper taped to the bottom of the shallow drawer.

I leaned closer. There were three numbers written on the square: 5/10/62.

"It looks like a date," I said. "May tenth, nineteen sixty-two. Maybe it's for something special the principal didn't want to forget, like a birthday or an anniversary."

"Oh." Hugh sounded disappointed. "I thought it might be a combination."

I hesitated. "Well, it could be, I guess. You mean like a combination for a locker?"

"Not a locker. A *safe*."

"A safe? What safe?"

Hugh squeezed past me and hurried over to a closet

door. "It's in here," he said in a hushed voice. I crossed the room and craned my neck to see around him as he stepped into the closet and reached up to pull a string dangling from the ceiling. A lightbulb flashed on with a pop, illuminating a cramped space lined with empty shelves on either side, and just like Hugh said, an old-timey safe sitting on top of another row of deep shelves on the back wall.

"Do you think you can open it?" he asked. "I'm not tall enough. The other day I got the chair from the office to stand on, but I still couldn't get it to work. I must not be doing it right."

"Wait, Hugh," I said. "This is crazy. You told me we weren't going to break any rules."

"But it's not like we're going to steal anything. I just want to take a quick look. It's the only way we can figure it out," he rushed on. "See, Hildy comes in the principal's office every night before she goes out searching. And sometimes she comes back again right before she goes to bed. After she went in the basement, she stayed in here for a really long time. I think she was locking whatever she found inside that safe!"

"But what if she catches us?"

"She won't. She won't even know we were here. Come on," Hugh pleaded. "You're the only one who can help me."

"Oh, all right," I said, scraping my sweaty hair back

from my face. "I'll try. But only if you stand out there and warn me if you hear somebody coming."

"Aye, aye!" Hugh saluted me and marched over to plant himself a few feet outside the closet.

I approached the safe and stood on my tiptoes to study the dial. Just last week my whole sixth-grade class had trooped down the street to the junior high to take a tour and practice opening lockers. I had opened mine on my very first try. But this dial was lots different from the one I had practiced on, and there was a brass lever next to it, instead of a skinny silver latch underneath.

"Five . . . ten . . . sixty-two," Hugh reminded me from the doorway.

I reached up, grasped the knob, and spun it around three times.

"Aren't you going to blow on your fingers first?" Hugh asked.

"Shush. Let me concentrate."

"Sorry. That's what I saw a guy do in a movie once and it worked for him."

"Five," I breathed. "Ten . . . sixty-two . . ." I bit down on my lip as I gripped the lever and tried twisting it left, then right. It wouldn't budge.

Hugh had stepped back inside the closet. "Try again," he said.

I let my arms dangle helplessly at my sides. "This is silly. It's not going to work."

"Pleeeease," he begged. "Just once more, and then we'll leave, I promise."

"One more try," I said. "And that's it!"

This time I wasn't even pretending to be precise as I spun the dial clockwise and counterclockwise and back again, so I was shocked when I grabbed the lever and it turned with a satisfying click.

Hugh wedged in beside me as I pulled the door open. "You did it!" he cried. I grasped the inside edge of the safe and stretched as tall as I could, straining to see all the way to the back of the steel compartment.

"Well?" Hugh demanded. "What's in there?"

"Nothing," I said. "It's empty."

"No way." He pushed in front of me. "Lift me up."

This was getting ridiculous. I had never met such a stubborn kid. I grabbed Hugh under his armpits and with a loud grunt hoisted him high enough to peer inside. He reached his arm into the safe and snatched at something.

"I told you!" Hugh crowed as I bumped him back onto the floor. He whirled around, waving an envelope in my face. "I told you it wasn't empty."

I don't know what I'd been expecting—a bag full of jewels maybe or a few stacks of hundred-dollar bills—but definitely something more than an old letter. Hugh examined the front of the envelope. "Here," he said, thrusting it toward me. "I'm not very good at reading other people's writing."

"Let's go out to the office where we can see better," I said.

Hugh watched my every move as I hurried to the window and held the envelope up to the sunlight. There were some foreign-looking stamps on the front, but no return address. "It's written to Miss Hildy Larson. Care of Mr. Jonathan Bonnycastle at the Fortune Consolidated School," I told Hugh, starting to catch a tingle of his excitement. "Hey, that's the teacher Hildy was telling me about." Fortunately the seal on the envelope had already been broken. I carefully opened the flap and pulled out a folded piece of tissue-thin paper. The handwriting inside was small and precise, penned in blue ink.

I glanced down at the signature at the bottom of the page. *Tom*. "It's from Hildy's brother," I said breathlessly. "She was talking about him this morning too."

Hugh gave an impatient little hop. "What's it say?"

I began reading out loud.

Dear Sis,
    Please don't read any further unless you're alone.

I stopped. I'd let an eight-year-old talk me into sneaking inside the principal's office, cracking a safe, and *now this*? "Hugh," I said queasily. "Maybe we shouldn't—"

"Keep going!" Hugh cried.

I let out a noisy sigh and kept going.

74

Our battalion is moving soon, so I'm rushing to get this posted. I may not be able to write again for a while.

I know Pop must have discovered his missing box by now. He's probably been beside himself trying to track down the culprit, right? Well, Sis, I have a confession to make. It wasn't a gang of thieves who stole Pop's treasure, or a hobo, or any other crazy notion he may have dreamed up. It was me—his own son.

I'm sorry, Hildy, but I had to! Before he frittered away the last thing he owned that was worth anything. I wanted there to be something left for you, just in case this war drags on, God forbid, and gets the best of yours truly.

You're probably wondering why I didn't just tell you all this before I shipped out. To be honest, I was worried you would be too softhearted to stand all of Pop's grieving and keep the secret safe. I knew it would be better to wait and tell you once the dust settled and once he'd had a little time to accept his loss.

It took ages for me to come up with a hiding place that Pop wouldn't find. Turns out Bonnycastle's the one who gave me the idea. Before I left, I stopped by FCS to say goodbye and suddenly, there it was, the best hiding place ever, right under good ole Bonny's nose!

I haven't shared any of this messy business with Bonny by the way. He doesn't know a thing about the treasure or that he's the one who gave me the bright idea about where to stash it. All I told him is that I would be *writing to you under his care—an important letter about family finances that I didn't want Pop to see—and he said he'd be glad to deliver my letter to you whenever it arrived.*

Once you read this, ask Bonny what he was doing when I came to say goodbye. Then you'll know exactly where to look for the box. Keep your nest egg there as long as you can, Hildy, and mum's the word!! I'll sleep better tonight knowing our fortune's safe and sound, waiting for you when you need it.

Your loving brother, Tom

I blinked down at Tom's signature, trying not to think about Dad again. "Poor Hildy," I whispered. "She told me her brother died in the Korean War. This might have been the last letter he wrote before he was killed."

"But I don't get it!" Hugh burst out. He scrubbed his hands through his hair until it was sticking up like dandelion fluff. "Her brother says he hid a box, but what was in it? We still don't know what Hildy's looking for."

I stared at the piece of stationery in my hands. "Yeah, but Hildy knows. And this letter must be her only key to finding the missing treasure. I bet that's why she locked the letter in the safe and why she keeps coming in here at night to study it for clues." I scanned the last two paragraphs. "So Tom and Mr. Bonnycastle must have been good friends. Tom says that he stopped by FCS—that's short for Fortune Consolidated School—to say goodbye. *'And suddenly, there it was,'"* I recited again, *"'the best hiding place ever, right under good ole Bonny's nose.'"*

I turned back to the office and leaned against the windowsill. "So according to this letter, the treasure's got to be here somewhere. But what about all of those *nos* Hildy wrote on the blackboards? It sounds like she searched the whole school and once she got to the basement, she gave up. I don't think she found anything down there. Otherwise the box would be in the safe too, right? And she wouldn't be worrying about stuff like electric bills."

"But she can't give up yet!" Hugh said. He dug in the side pocket of his shorts for his index card and fished the pencil from behind his ear. "We should be taking notes. So we can help her solve the mystery." Then before I could stop him, he plunked himself down on the swivel chair next to the desk and started writing.

I groaned under my breath and glanced down at the letter again. There was a date at the top that I hadn't noticed before. June 30, 1950—the same year Hildy had graduated from high school and the very same month she had been crowned Fortune's button queen. *When had Tom been killed?* I wondered. Hildy had looked so carefree in her parade picture, smiling and waving to the crowd. I was sure it must have been taken before she found out her brother was gone forever.

Hugh twirled his chair around to face me. "What does that one word mean?" he asked. *"Frittered* . . . Whatever that thing Hildy's father was doing with the treasure."

"I think it means he was wasting it," I said. "Basically, Pop doesn't sound like he was very good with money." Hugh twirled back to the desk and hunched over his index card again.

I folded Tom's letter along its worn crease and slid it back into the envelope. "Come on, Hugh. I'm serious. Let's go."

The words had barely left my mouth when I heard the crunch of tires on gravel in the parking lot outside the window. "Somebody just pulled up!" I yelped as I darted away from the window. "Hurry! It's probably your mom back from the store."

I lurched for the closet. My hands were shaking as I pushed the letter inside the safe, slammed the door closed, and turned the lever. I almost forgot to switch the light off, but then scrambled back to yank the string. When I burst out of the closet, Hugh was on his knees peering over the edge of the windowsill. "Dramn it," I heard him say.

I froze halfway to the door. "What's going on?"

"The carnivores are here," Hugh said. "And they don't look very happy."

NINE

I DIDN'T GET A SINGLE GLIMPSE of Hildy's relatives. By the time they rang the buzzer, I was already sprinting up to the second floor and Hugh was scurrying to the library to file his notes in the card catalog and wait for Mine to get back. I spent the afternoon in Room 26, nibbling on my smushed peanut butter sandwiches, thinking about the missing treasure, and trying to decide what to do next. Hopefully Hildy had forgotten all about me in the flurry of her company arriving. To keep from reminding her, I made up my mind to stay out of sight for as long as possible.

At least my window looked out on the old baseball field, and watching Garrett helped to distract me for a while. He had made a wall of shells around the diamond, and now he had a large coil of rope slung over his shoulder. He marched to the center of the open space and pounded a stake into the ground. After that, there was a lot of pacing back and forth, kicking up little clouds of dust with his giant boots and stopping to stroke his beard. I finally turned away from the window, shaking my head. It was hard to imagine how Garrett was going to turn the rest of those sloppy piles of shells into any sort of tourist attraction.

I had just stretched out on my cot to read another chapter of *Little Women* when Hugh came tearing into the room. "Hey, can you come help us with dinner?" he panted. He held up his pointer finger. It was wrapped in a bloody Band-Aid. "I cut myself trying to peel potatoes and Mine's acting like she might have one of those, you know, those nervous breakdown things."

"Where's Hildy?" I asked. I pushed myself up from the cot. "Isn't she helping?"

"No. She's still showing her son around the museum. Mine wouldn't want Hildy's help anyway. They get kind of cranky when they cook together."

I checked my watch for the tenth time that afternoon. It was three-thirty. If Hildy spotted me in the kitchen, I'd just have to say Mom was probably on her way and pray that Nora didn't have to work tonight in case I needed to make another fake phone call. I reached in my pocket to squeeze my new lucky charm and followed Hugh down-stairs.

When we arrived in the kitchen, Mine had an oven rack pulled out and was staring down at a partly cooked slab of meat like it was a dead possum that had just landed in her pan. "Oh, hey, Ren," she said. Her voice was tense and her cheeks were blazing. "Any idea how long you should cook a rump roast? Or what temperature I should be using?"

I winced. "Gosh, I'm not sure. Is roast anything like meat loaf? I think my mom cooks most stuff at 350."

Mine swung her dreadlock ponytail over her shoulder and bent down to shove the pan back into the oven. "I'm going to turn this baby up to 425." She twisted one of the knobs behind the burners on top. "Just to be sure it's done in time. I've never seen such a bloody piece of meat."

I took over peeling potatoes while Hugh sat on the counter next to me banging his heels against the cabinets. Mine started to make a salad, then realized that some of the vegetables she had bought at the store were missing. "They probably forgot to put one of my bags in the cart," she grumbled as she left to check in her car. "I hope everybody likes lettuce."

She had only been gone a minute when Hugh and I heard Hildy arguing with somebody out in the cafeto-rium. Hugh stopped bumping his heels and I froze with my potato peeler in midair. "Of course people will pay five bucks to get in, Jack," Hildy was saying. "Five dollars would be a bargain! Didn't I tell you those priss-pots at the historical society are banging my door down trying to get a look at my collection? If they can charge admission at their rinky-dink museum, why can't I?"

Hugh stared back at me, his eyes round.

"It's ridiculous, Mother," Hildy's son answered, his voice bristling with impatience. "You could have moved to a nice retirement center with what you made selling your antiques store in Bellefield and your old home in Fortune. But, instead, you're spending your last savings on this outlandish venture. And what about all that debris piled in the gym? It's a fire hazard. If the fire marshal ever finds his way out here, you'll be shut down. I knew you'd been collecting button memorabilia over the years, but good grief, I had no idea how much you had socked away at your shop and in that old barn behind the house. Forgive me, but how in the world do you think you can pull this off on your own?"

"I'm not on my own," Hildy snapped. "I've got Garrett. And Mayor Joy's back. He says he's not going out on any more jobs this summer and he wants to help me."

"That's another thing. Who are all these characters that you're taking under your wing? You're charging them peanuts. They're using you, Mother. You should at least be conducting some sort of screening process or background check before you roll out the welcome wagon for anyone who happens to wander through."

Like me, I thought uneasily. I set the potato peeler down on the counter.

"Listen, son," Hildy was saying. "You're not going to talk me out of this. I'm an old, old woman and I think I've earned the right to do what I want. It's been a dream of mine for the last fifty years."

There was a long pause, and when Hildy's son finally answered, his voice had quieted. Before I could stop him, Hugh slid down from the counter, darted to the side of the serving window, and peeked around the edge. I couldn't resist tiptoeing over to the opposite side so I could hear too. "I'm well acquainted with how stubborn you can be when you set your mind to something, Mother," the man was saying. "I expected you'd react this way so I've already been thinking about how to help you get a handle on the situation. I need to head back to Des Moines tonight, right after dinner, but I've decided to leave Tucker here with you."

"*What?*" Hildy squawked. "For how long?"

"The whole summer."

I glanced over at Hugh. He was pressed up against the window frame, his face bright with anticipation. Maybe Tucker would be the friend he'd been waiting for.

Hildy, on the other hand, didn't sound so happy with the idea. "Jack!" she cried. "Have you lost your wits? No thirteen-year-old boy wants to spend the summer with his grandmother, stuck out in the country without any friends nearby. Tucker will be bored silly! You saw how disappointed he was a few minutes ago when I told him we don't have a hookup for that Internet business out here."

"It's already decided, Mother. Tucker won't have a chance to be bored. He'll be working. There aren't many jobs available for someone his age so I'm going to pay him to work here in that . . . that museum of yours. He'll be earning real wages and I expect you to treat him like any other employee—"

We didn't get to hear the rest. Mine came banging through the swinging door. "Hey, what are you guys doing?" she asked, narrowing her eyes as she glanced back and forth between the two of us.

"Nothing," Hugh said. "We thought we heard a funny noise out there." But the cafetorium had fallen silent. Hildy and her son must have moved on as soon as they heard voices. And Mine was too preoccupied with the search for her missing vegetables—they weren't in her car either—to care what we'd been up to.

The next hour was a blur of trying to decide things like how long to boil the potatoes and which tablecloths we should use to cover the picnic tables and how many places we should set. At first Mine said eight. Then Hugh told her that the Mayor was back from his latest trucking run. "Oh, and what about you, Ren?" Mine asked. "Your mom was supposed to come and get you, right? Or did you decide to stay for dinner?"

When I fumbled for an answer Mine said, "Either way's fine. Why don't you set an extra place just in case?"

I scurried back and forth from the kitchen to the cafetorium, keeping my eye out for Hildy as I set the table with her hodgepodge collection of dishes and silverware. My palms were so sweaty that I almost dropped the slippery water glasses I was carrying. I wanted to run back upstairs to hide out in my room. But how was I supposed to escape now without making a scene?

Once the roast was done and Mine had given up trying to mash more lumps out of the potatoes, she sent Hugh to round everyone up for dinner. Hildy's son was the first to appear. Instead of coming to the table though, he stood near the entrance to the gym introducing himself and shaking hands with each of the tenants as they arrived. "Hello. How are you? Jack Baxter. Good to meet you," he kept saying. He sounded like a politician running for office, and he looked sort of like one too, with his helmet of carefully combed hair and his starched khakis and button-down shirt.

"I'm Clarissa," Sister Loud bellowed as she shook Mr. Baxter's hand. "And this is my sister, Colette." Sister Soft said something polite, but I couldn't hear exactly what. Garrett had arrived in a fresh change of clothes. It was hard not to stare. He was even taller and burlier than he had appeared from my perch in Room 26. He reminded me of a Viking, like he should have been wearing boots to his knees and one of those hats with horns, instead of flip-flops and his bushy gold hair slicked down with water. Mr. Baxter looked like a dwarf beside him as they stood exchanging stiff hellos.

Hildy appeared from behind the curtains just as Mayor Joy walked in. He dashed over to escort her down the stairs of the stage. She had put on a fresh coat of lipstick in fire-engine red, but she seemed frazzled as she crossed the cafetorium leaning on the Mayor's arm. Her eyebrows shot up when she spotted me coming out of the kitchen carrying a bowl of mashed potatoes.

"Ren!" she cried, letting go of the Mayor's arm. "You're still here! Wasn't your mother supposed to pick you up this afternoon?"

I cringed apologetically. "I'm really sorry, Hildy. My mom's never on time, and Mine said I could stay for dinner. Would that be okay?"

"Oh, I suppose so," she said with a helpless shrug. "But we'll have to be sure to listen for the buzzer." I nodded and quickly delivered the potatoes to the table. Mr. Baxter and the others were starting to make their way over.

"Now where'd Tucker get off to?" Hildy asked as she seated herself at the head.

"He'll be along any minute, Mother," Mr. Baxter told

her. "He's getting the rest of his things out of the car." He hesitated next to the table, frowning down at the wooden picnic benches that were pulled up on either side. Then, with a sigh, he squeezed himself into a spot on the end next to his mother.

When I slipped back into the kitchen, Mine was crouched over the roast with a fork and a carving knife. "This meat is as tough as shoe leather," she moaned under her breath. "I can barely cut into it. I probably shouldn't even serve it." Hugh stood quietly patting his mother's back as he peered down at the grayish-brown hunks on the platter.

I ran over and opened the refrigerator. "Look!" I said, trying to sound cheerful. "You've got ketchup. And A.1. Sauce! My dad loves this stuff." I grabbed the bottles from the door of the fridge. "No one will care if their meat's a little dry."

"Thank you, Ren," she said as she set down the carving knife and wiped the back of her wrist across her shiny forehead. The diamond in her nose glinted. "What would we have done without you today?" I couldn't help feeling pleased with myself, especially when Hugh flashed me his own thankful smile.

"All right." Mine squared her shoulders and reached up to tighten her bandanna around her frizzy bundle of dreads. "Might as well get this over with."

TEN

EVERYONE WAS SEATED and waiting when Mine and Hugh and I finally came out of the kitchen with the platter of meat and every bottle of sauce we could find in the refrigerator. I hung back for a second, trying to figure out where I should sit.

"Come down here, honey," Hildy called, pointing to the small space between her son and Sister Loud, straight across from Tucker. He must have arrived while we were finishing up in the kitchen. I could feel him staring as I threaded myself into the open spot on the picnic bench, trying not to knock up against anyone with my knees or the bottles of ketchup and A.1. "Everybody, this is Ren Winningham," Hildy announced. "Ren is"—there was an awkward pause—"visiting us from Bellefield."

Thank goodness Mine jumped in with her own introductions. She welcomed Mr. Baxter and Tucker, then quickly started babbling out apologies for the plain salad and the tough roast.

Carefully, I lifted my gaze. Tucker had a swoop of long black bangs and blue eyes—or at least one of his eyes was blue. I couldn't see the other one hidden behind his hair. He wore a leather cord around his neck, strung with a silver bead, and he seemed edgier than the boys I was used to. Maybe he would have been cute if he hadn't looked so miserable. Judging from his dreary expression and slouched shoulders, it wasn't hard to guess how he felt about spending his summer at the school.

"This is wonderful, Mine," Mayor Joy called down the table as he tried to shake a stubborn dollop of mashed potatoes off the serving spoon onto his plate. "It's been two weeks since I had a home-cooked meal."

"And what do you do for a living, Mr. Joy?" Mr. Baxter asked.

"I'm a trucker," the Mayor said. "I was a farmer too until a few months ago. Had a little place on the edge of town, but a developer came knocking and made an offer I couldn't refuse."

"Elton's bunking out back for the time being," Hildy told her son. "He fixed up a nice little room in the old tool-shed and there's plenty of room for Wayne out there."

Mr. Baxter cocked his head. "Wayne?"

"My donkey," the Mayor replied. "We've been together for a long time."

I wiped my mouth with my napkin, holding back the urge to giggle and sneak another look across the table.

Hildy had reached out to pat the Mayor's hand. "Elton probably moved to Fortune and took over as mayor about the time you left home, Jack. How many years has it been, Elton?"

"Climbing up on forty," the Mayor said.

Mr. Baxter looked amused. "I'm interested to hear why you'd want to serve that long . . . in a town like Fortune that's been on its way out for as long as I can remember."

Mayor Joy looked surprised at the question. "Why, it was the biggest honor of my life getting elected," he said. "I was one of the first black men to be voted mayor in this part of the country." He shook his head. "That's something you don't give up on that easily, even if your town wants to give up the ghost before you do." He laughed and tucked his napkin into his collar. "We've got our council meeting this week. You're coming, aren't you, Clarissa?"

"Of course!" Sister Loud fired out next to my ear, making me wince. "You know I never miss a meeting."

Mr. Baxter raised one eyebrow. "You've kept the town council going too? And how many people are left on this council of yours?"

"There're four of us," the Mayor told him. His tone had

turned a little less jolly. "We've got more to discuss than you would think—like those developers in the area and your mother's museum. We're hoping we can breathe a little life back into this old town of ours."

Mr. Baxter's jaw clenched as he thumped the bottom of the A.1. bottle with the heel of his hand. "Oh, I see. So the council was probably involved in convincing my mother to buy this dilapidated old place."

"That's enough, Jack," Hildy scolded before the Mayor had a chance to answer. "Elton and the council had nothing to do with my decision." The table went quiet as we all busied ourselves with trying to saw through the slabs of meat on our plates. I managed to hack off a corner and chew my way through a tiny bite. Mine was right. Shoe leather.

Mr. Baxter cleared his throat and leaned forward. "So, Garrett," he began, "I took a walk around the property before dinner and got a glimpse of your project out back. Mother says you're using all those shells to construct some sort of maze."

Garrett smoothed his beard with his napkin. "Not a maze, sir. It's a labyrinth." His voice was the kind that made you want to listen, low and rumbly, and he had one of those cool British accents, which took me by surprise. Hugh had said that Garrett used to fix up old castles and churches in England, but he never mentioned that Garrett had come from there too.

Mr. Baxter spent a long time chewing. Then he took a few more seconds to swallow, with his Adam's apple moving up and down. "You'll have to enlighten me," he continued at last, reaching for his glass of water. "What's the difference between a maze and a labyrinth?"

"Completely different purposes," Garrett said. "Mazes are designed to be a puzzle, to confound the visitor and entertain. But it's impossible to make a wrong turn in a labyrinth. There's only one path in and one path out."

"And what would the purpose be in *that*?" Mr. Baxter asked.

The corners of Garrett's mustache lifted in a slow smile. "You'll have to walk it when I'm done and see for yourself."

"Doesn't really sound like my sort of thing." Mr. Baxter eyed the brown puddle of sauce on his plate with distaste. "And it seems to me there might be more pressing jobs around this place than moving ten tons of shells around in a circle."

Hildy set down her fork, ready to intervene. But Garrett beat her to it. "No need to worry, sir," he said lightly. "I've been saving my labyrinth work for the weekends and after hours." Then Garrett glanced over at Hugh, obviously searching for a way to lift the mood. "Plus my mate Hugh here has been lending me a hand whenever he's available. Right, Hugh? We'll be done in no time at all."

When Hugh nodded happily, Mr. Baxter pounced like

a cat after a mouse. "And where do you go to school, Hugh? Over in Bellefield?"

Hugh leaned his head to one side, thinking. "I don't really go to school anymore," he said. Then he turned to look at Mine. "Do I?" Before she had a chance to reply, Hugh let out a hiccupy laugh. "That's kind of funny, huh? I live in a school, but I don't have to go to school anymore."

Mine straightened uneasily in her seat. "Well, of course you have to go to school, Hugh," she said with a flustered smile. "We're going to start homeschooling in a few weeks, remember? Once you're done with summer vacation."

Now Mr. Baxter was the one setting his fork down with a loud clink, and I stole a glance at Tucker just in time to see him spit something into his napkin. Of course that's when he happened to look across the table, and our eyes finally met as he was trying to lower his hand from his mouth without being noticed. I glanced away, mortified, thinking that this dinner couldn't possibly get any worse—until I spotted someone standing in the doorway across the room.

My mother.

The options raced through my head. I needed to leap up from my seat or pretend to choke on Mine's roast . . . something . . . anything . . . to avoid the awful scene that was coming. I could see it etched across Mom's face as she stalked toward us. I had never seen her so furious, with her arms rigid and her fists clenched at her sides. Even her hair looked like it belonged to someone else. Instead of wearing it loose around her shoulders like always, she had scraped every strand back in a tight knot.

"And who have we here?" Mr. Baxter asked. Still, I couldn't seem to move. When Hildy twisted in her seat, and Tucker and the Mayor and everyone else turned to see, I opened my mouth to say something, but no words came out.

Mom stopped a few feet behind Hildy, staring at me. Her neck was blotchy, and I could see her chest rising up and down.

"Oh, hello there," Hildy said as she stood up from the table. "You must be Ren's mother. I'm sorry we didn't hear the buzzer. How'd you manage to get in?"

"The front door wasn't latched all the way," Mom answered in an icy voice. "So I took the liberty of letting myself in. Are you Mrs. Baxter?"

Hildy nodded. "That's me. You can call me Hildy." She reached out her hand.

Mom ignored it. "I've come to get my daughter," she said. "But first, can you explain to me why *on earth* you would allow a twelve-year-old girl to run away from her family and hide out in this"—she let her gaze roam over the table and the stage with its dusty velvet curtains— "this place . . . surrounded by complete strangers . . . without the slightest effort to notify me?"

"Twelve?" Hildy spluttered with an appalled glance in

my direction. "She said she was fourteen. And of course I notified you! I called as soon as Ren showed up on my doorstep! And you told me *very clearly* that it was fine for her to stay and that you'd pick her up this afternoon. Frankly, I expected you much earlier than this."

"What?" Mom blinked her eyes closed, shaking her head in confusion. "That's ridiculous. We've never spoken. In fact I'd never even heard of you until about an hour and a half ago when my older daughter finally broke down and told me that Ren was hiding out at some sort of rooming house in Fortune—run by a woman named Mrs. Baxter."

Somehow I had found my way to my feet, and now I lurched past Hildy to take hold of my mother's arm. "Mom, it's okay," I pleaded. "I'll explain everything later. Let's just go." But my mother wasn't planning on going anywhere yet. She pulled her arm away and held up her palm as stiff as a stop sign in front of my face.

"Well, then who in the devil was I talking to?" Hildy demanded. "Whoever it was said she was Ren's mother!" Everyone was staring at me now, their faces caught in the gold light that had come slanting through the row of windows across the shabby room.

"Ren?" Hildy asked.

"That was my sister you talked to," my voice creaked out. "Nora. She pretended to be Mom."

My mother's face had gone pale. *"What?"* she gasped.

"Ren, how could you? How could Nora?" She shook her head in dismay. "Do you have any idea how worried I've been? As soon as I read your note last night, I wanted to go get you at Allison's, but it was late and I decided it'd be better for both of us if I gave you some time to calm down. Then I waited as long as I could to go over this morning, figuring you girls would want to sleep in. I nearly flipped when Carol told me you weren't there. Nora was at work all day, but when I called her, she told me not to worry."

Mom's eyes flashed with anger. "She said you were probably hiding out at some other friend's house. So I contacted everybody I could think of. Kelly, Emma, all the girls on your soccer team, Uncle Spence, everybody! By this afternoon I was in a complete panic. I called Nora back at work and that's when she confessed you had called last night." Then Mom let out a shuddery breath and turned to Hildy. "I apologize. Nora neglected to tell me she had spoken with you and played such a thoughtless trick, but at least she gave me the number here. I must have called a dozen times, trying to find out your address. But I kept getting your voice mail. Didn't you get my messages?"

Hildy was patting at her pockets, the same way she had last night. "I had that darn thing with me this morning," she said, her voice faint. "How'd you find me then?"

"I called the sheriff's office," Mom said.

"The sheriff!" Hildy squawked in alarm.

My mother nodded. "Thank goodness the deputy I spoke to knew about this place and told me how to get here."

"Good land," Hildy muttered. "There goes my reputation."

"I'm sorry," I whispered. I could feel little pricks gathering behind my eyes as I met Hildy's sad gaze. I wheeled toward the table. "I'm sorry, everybody," I said, with my throat welling. "I never meant to cause so much trouble."

Hugh looked like he might be on the verge of tears too. So he'd been right after all. I'd never come back to visit like I said I would—just like Mine's last boyfriend. How could I ever show my face at the school again after today?

"Please, Mom," I begged. "Come on. We need to let them finish dinner. And I've got to go upstairs and get my stuff." This time Mom followed along as I tugged her toward the door to the gym.

Before we had even made it over the threshold, I could hear Mr. Baxter blustering away. "What in the world was that all about? Mother? Who was that girl?"

I couldn't bear to hear Hildy's answer. I dropped Mom's arm and fled down the hall.

ELEVEN

I WAS GROUNDED FOR LIFE—or that's how Mom made it sound the next day when she was on the phone with Allison's mom. I had cracked my bedroom door open to listen. "I'm sorry, Carol," I overheard Mom say. "Ren won't be able to go to Adventure Bay with Allison and the other girls after all . . . No, sorry, next week won't work either. I'm afraid you'll have to go ahead without her. Ren's going to be sticking close to home for a while."

I banged my door shut and didn't crack it open again until I heard my sister going back and forth to the bathroom. Nora was grounded too, but at least she got to leave the house for work since Mom said she'd make an exception for official employment.

"Pssst," I hissed at Nora when she was on her way downstairs. She rolled her eyes, but turned and followed me into my room. "I feel like we did that whole thing for nothing," I said after I had shut the door and thrown myself on my bed. "Mom won't even admit that this was all her fault in the first place. She says that she *did* work late the other night and she only took a quick break to go out to dinner because she thought I'd still be at Allison's pool party. *Supposedly* Rick called her at the last minute."

Nora didn't answer at first. She bent down to tie her pink Converse sneakers. I was jealous of her waitress uniform—khaki shorts and a hot-pink polo shirt with her name stitched in green across the front.

"So what do we do now?" I asked.

Nora stood up, swinging her smooth brown ponytail over her shoulder. "What do *we* do now?" she repeated, so bitterly that my mouth dropped open. "How about *we* do *nothing*? Listen, Ren. I can't believe I let you drag me into that crazy plan of yours. You went way too far. And now I'm grounded too, for agreeing to cover for you."

I stared at Nora. "Why are you acting like you don't care all of a sudden?"

"Of course I care," she said. "But you need to stop thinking you can change things between Mom and Dad. They're either going to work it out on their own or they're not."

"How's Dad supposed to work things out if he's stuck out in a desert somewhere thousands of miles away?"

"The thing is, Ren, we can't *tell* Mom how to feel. We can't *make* her want to stay married to Dad if she doesn't love him that way anymore."

My breath caught. Nora might as well have plunged an arrow into me and twisted it. "But she *does* love him!" I cried. "She said so . . . in his birthday card."

Nora heaved out a sigh. "I can't think about this right now. I have to go or I'll be late for work."

I watched helplessly as she slipped through my door. What was going on? Was I the only one who hadn't jumped ship on our family?

Mom called me down for lunch a few minutes later, and I decided to find out once and for all. When I came into the kitchen she was standing at the sink washing dishes, and a turkey sandwich made exactly the way I liked it—toasted with honey mustard and pickles—sat waiting for me in my spot at the island. "So just tell me," I said to the back of my mother's head as I hoisted myself onto the bar stool and took a bite of her peace offering. "Are you and Dad getting a divorce or what?"

Mom's shoulders went as limp as the dishrag she was wringing dry. She gazed out at the backyard beyond the kitchen window. "I don't know, Ren," she replied, "but that stunt you pulled this weekend isn't making things any easier for anybody." She turned to face me, leaning against the sink with her arms crossed. "Honestly, if you were going to run away, why didn't you go to Uncle

Spence's or one of your friends' houses? Why would you pick that run-down old school with all those bizarre characters hanging around? Who knows what could have happened if I hadn't come when I did?"

"They're not bizarre," I said hotly. "Hildy's grandson is spending his whole summer there. Do you think his dad would let him stay if it wasn't safe?" Each time I thought of the school felt like a fresh slap. All night long I had tossed and turned, picturing those shocked faces at Hildy's dinner table staring up at me. I'd never been so mortified. But even worse, I'd never get to go back—to finish exploring the school and help Hugh solve the mystery of the missing treasure.

"Did you call Dad and tell him what happened?" I asked.

"Of course not. What good would that have done? He would have been worried sick, with no way to help."

I pushed my plate away. "I bet you didn't call him because he would have asked why I ran away and then you would've had to tell him about Rick."

"Ren." Mom looked up at the ceiling in frustration. "There's nothing to tell about Rick. The issues between your father and me started a long time ago—way before Rick ever moved to town. And like I've told you before, Rick and I are *friends*. That's it!"

"Yeah, and you also told me you weren't going to hang out with him anymore!"

"I know I did," Mom said quietly. "And that's something I *do* want to apologize for—for agreeing to such a silly promise. It would be ridiculous for me to tell Rick that we can't be friends. That would imply that there's something going on between us, and there's not."

"Oh, really?" I scoffed.

Mom grabbed the dishrag again and began scrubbing at an invisible spot on the counter in front of me. "Honestly, Ren, this has got to stop. It isn't healthy, this silly obsessing over Rick. I can't have you sitting around here all summer monitoring my every move and brooding over whether it means anything. You need to keep busy. That's why I decided to sign you up for that camp that we talked about. I sent the form in a few days ago and I was just waiting for a good time to tell you."

"What?" I stiffened on my stool. "What camp?"

Mom didn't answer. She turned back to the sink to rinse out the dishrag.

"No, Mom," I moaned over the sound of the running water. "You didn't. Not SAG. I already told you I didn't want to go!"

SAG. The Summer Academy for the Gifted. By invitation only. Guaranteed to stimulate talented young minds . . . and guaranteed to be just as terrible as it sounded. I already knew two kids in my class who had signed up the day after their letters arrived. Olivia Pasternak and

Arnold Morales. No way was I spending five weeks of my summer with a boy whose favorite hobbies were topping his latest Rubik's Cube time and turning his eyelids inside out.

"Please, Mom," I said desperately as I hurried around the island. "I'm already signed up for soccer camp at the end of July. And what about swimming lessons? I'll be plenty busy." Mom's profile remained stony. "I could even do those art classes at the rec center. Anything! But I'm not going to that stupid SAG!"

Mom whirled around to face me. "Listen, young lady. You are in no position to tell me what you will and won't do this summer. You're signed up for the Academy and that's it. The bus picks up kids at the junior high tomorrow at nine a.m. and you're going to be on it!"

Young lady was a sure sign that there was no use arguing anymore. I stormed back to my room and stayed huddled on my bed, scribbling in my little-kid diary with the gold latch and tiny key that somebody had given me a few birthdays ago. I'd barely used up twenty pages. And most of those were this year, since I only wrote in it when I had a crush on somebody or when I was mad.

But that afternoon I filled up ten whole pages on Mom and Rick and SAG, and then I found myself thinking about Fortune again and filling another page with doodles of the school and Wayne the donkey and the leopard cats. The hours limped by until Mom finally flung open my door and ordered me to go "get some fresh air" and to weed the flower beds out front while I was at it. After the dim light of my bedroom, the sky was such a dazzling blue that I felt like a groundhog poking out of its hole as I sat in a scraggly patch of weeds, ripping the tops off dandelions. I was trying not to think about the school or my friends swooshing down waterslides when a voice called from the sidewalk.

"Hey, Ren."

I didn't turn around.

"I fixed your bike tire for you."

Now I'd have to talk to him. I slowly looked up from my weeding, making my eyes into slits. Rick was already walking my bike up the driveway. He was decked out in his wraparound sunglasses and flashy running gear and he had Chauncey, his Portuguese water dog, with him. I stood up and went down to meet him halfway. "Thanks," I muttered as I took the handlebars. Chauncey whimpered and lunged toward me, but I willed myself not to pet him or meet Rick's eye. Unfortunately Chauncey was about the cutest dog I had ever seen—a squirmy black puff with markings like white socks on his feet. I had loved playing with him before Rick's secret mission to steal my mother became not so secret.

I started pushing my bike back up the driveway. "I'm

glad you're home safe," Rick said behind me. Mom must have been giving him a minute-by-minute update on my whereabouts yesterday. He raised his voice over Chauncey's whining. "Your mother was really worried about you, you know."

I could feel the blood rushing to my face as I parked my bike by the flower bed. It was something Dad would have said if he were here right now. And Rick had no business standing in our driveway trying to sound like my dad.

"Yes, I did know that," I shot out before I could stop myself. "And did *you* know my father gets home from Afghanistan in thirty-four days? He's moving in here again as soon as he gets back."

I could see how shocked Rick was, even through his mirrored sunglasses. But he didn't have time to answer. The screen door creaked open behind me and Mom stepped out on the porch. I quickly bent down, pretending to focus on a stubborn hunk of crabgrass.

"Hey there, Rick," she called. "You fixed Ren's bike already? That's wonderful." I let out the breath I'd been holding. She hadn't heard me.

"No problem," Rick answered in a tight voice.

"Nice day for a run," Mom added.

Rick nodded. "Sure is. Well, I better get going. Chauncey and I are cranking it up to twelve miles today."

I smiled slyly to myself as he turned and jogged off. *Ha.* I didn't need Nora's help after all. I could get rid of Rick on my own.

· · · · ·

Dad must have known somehow that I needed to hear his voice that night. He called just before bedtime, and Mom pressed the receiver against her sweatshirt before she handed me the phone. "No drama," she whispered with a warning finger. "Your father doesn't need that right now."

I gave a snippy nod as I took the phone and went to flop on the couch in the dark living room. "Hi, Daddy," I said.

"Hey, Schnitzel," Dad said, sighing like he had been waiting a million years to talk to me. I had to pinch the inside corners of my eyelids so I wouldn't start crying. Who knows why Dad called me Schnitzel? He had been calling me that forever. I didn't even know what a Schnitzel was. Why hadn't I ever asked?

Sometimes the phone connection with Dad was so bad that his voice came through all tinny and muffled, like he was calling from the bottom of the ocean. But tonight he sounded like he was in the next room. "How you doing?" he asked me.

I kept my eyes squeezed shut. "Good." He let out a hoot

when I told him about my award, and I forced a cheery note into my voice when he asked me about my plans for the summer. "I'm signed up for some camps," I told him. "And I'm going to go over to Uncle Spence's as much as I can to keep Blue company. But what about you?" I asked, rushing to change the subject. I wanted to tell him about SAG, but I also knew it would be selfish to waste all our phone time with my complaining. "What are you doing today?"

"Well, I'm heading over to get breakfast in a few minutes, which is sure to be a treat." It was ten hours later where Dad was. I could picture him running his hand over his bristly crew cut, breaking into a crooked smile. He had told me stories about the mess hall food before, about how the scrambled eggs always tasted sandy and the soldiers had contests to see who could figure out what was in the latest mystery meat stew.

I started to ask Dad if his unit was going out on patrol that day, but then stopped myself. I didn't really want to know. "Are you being extra careful, Dad?" I asked instead.

"Absolutely, Schnitzel," he soothed. "Hey, we're in the homestretch, remember? In just a few weeks the four of us will be sitting on a blanket by the river having a picnic. I'm putting in my order now for those brownies of yours, okay? The ones with the caramel and the marshmallows?"

"I'll make you a double batch," I told him with the word *four* echoing in my ear. Suddenly, Nora was standing in front of me, holding her hand out for the phone, and for the first time this year, I was glad when my turn to talk to Dad was done.

TWELVE

MAYBE I SHOULD HAVE LEFT MY BUTTON BLANK at home on Monday morning. So far, it had failed me as a good luck charm, and by Monday afternoon I was convinced that the blank I had picked up in Hildy's museum was a complete dud.

SAG was even worse than I thought it would be. The bus ride took forever. We had to make stops in three other towns in order to scrape up enough kids to fill a classroom at the community college. And our counselor at the Academy was a short, bouncy guy with gelled hair who asked us to call him Stretch and made us spend the whole morning playing embarrassing icebreaker games. We started out with: If you were a fruit or a vegetable, what would you be? I knew I was in for a long month when Arnold Morales said, "I'd be an orange because I'm always ready to be squeezed."

When Ollie Pasternak said she'd be a tomato because it's well-rounded—technically a fruit but also accepted as a vegetable—Stretch gave her a high five like she had just scored a game-winning basket.

I didn't get a high five for wanting to be a kumquat. "Why?" Stretch asked, drumming his fingers on his chin. His eyes darted to my name tag. "Ren. Why a kumquat?"

"Because"—I shrugged, but then decided to be honest— "it's a really cool-sounding word?" Stretch nodded politely and went on to the next person.

As if the fruit/vegetable exercise hadn't been enough torture, he brought out two fat red balloons and challenged us to keep them both in the air without using our hands. Obviously that meant a lot of blowing, which isn't very fun when you're in a circle with thirteen strangers, including a couple who have really bad breath.

After lunch, Stretch said it was time for our first project. We were going to design imaginary cities. "No holds barred!" he sang out, throwing his hands in the air. "Be bold! Be creative! You want your city to be on the planet Mars? Go for it! Just make sure you and your partner figure out how to get water and oxygen up there. Oh, and don't forget you're gonna need one heck of a cooling system."

I almost stopped listening when he mentioned partners. Group activities weren't my favorite, and of course Stretch had come up with a particularly inventive way for how we would pair up. He passed out seven cards labeled with different state names and seven more cards listing their matching capitals. I got Alaska.

I was so nervous about who my partner would be, I suddenly couldn't remember Alaska's capital, even though I'd been able to recite capital cities as easy as the ABC's back when I was in fourth grade. My hopes fell when Seraphina, the one girl I might have wanted to team up with, held up her card. *Topeka.* At least I remembered enough to know that Topeka went with Kansas, not Alaska.

Then all at once, Arnold was marching toward me. "*Juneau* who your partner is?" he asked with a toothy grin as he flipped over his card. I blinked my eyes closed and forced out a weak smile.

Juneau. The capital of Alaska. How could I forget?

Mom didn't feel the least bit sorry for me that week. As soon as she came home from work each day, I'd tell her my latest SAG horror story—how awful it was riding on the hot bus and partnering with Arnold, who left sweat prints on all our papers and insisted that our imaginary city should be underground with a pipeline that would transform hazardous gases into a renewable energy source. "And he wants to call it Moleville," I wailed. "Who would want to live in a place called *Moleville?*"

Mom thought it was all hilarious. "This is good for you, Ren," she said with a laugh on Friday evening after I had poured out the unpleasant details of our field trip that day—a tour of the local dump and recycling center. "This is what they call character building."

"Who's *they*?" I muttered, but she didn't answer. She was too preoccupied with making cookies for some sort of fund-raiser at the farmers' market the next morning. I had to ask about ten questions before I finally figured out who the bake sale was for.

The Bellefield Volunteer Rescue Squad.

"What's wrong?" Nora asked when I came stomping upstairs.

"Rick Alert," I snarled as I slammed my bedroom door.

• • • • •

On Saturday morning Allison called to see if I could come over to swim that afternoon. Mom shook her head back and forth as I held the phone to my stomach mouthing *pleeeeaaase.* "Sorry, Allison." I heaved a sigh into the phone. "I'm still grounded."

But at least Mom budged enough to say I could ride my bike over to check on Old Blue while she was off helping at the bake sale. Uncle Spence liked to sleep till noon on the weekends, so I didn't even bother ringing his door-bell when I arrived. I went straight to the backyard and found Blue lying in front of his plastic doghouse with his chin on his paws. As soon as he heard my voice, he sprang to his feet, let out an overjoyed coonhound howl, and began hurling himself at the chain-link fence surround-ing his narrow run. Once I had unlatched the door and squeezed through, it took another fifteen minutes of wrig-gling and licking and jumping before Blue would sit still while I knelt in the dirt stroking his glossy blue-black ears and the tan spots over his sad eyes.

I was longing to let him out of the cramped pen, but I couldn't find a leash or a single piece of rope in Uncle Spence's shed. Luckily I had remembered to bring a baggie full of cut-up hot dogs, and Blue's nose got a good workout sniffing and snuffling around my pocket. I fi-nally gave in and fed him most of the bag. The last few pieces I threw in the deepest corners of his doghouse so he'd be distracted rooting under his blanket and I wouldn't have to see him staring mournfully through the fence as I made my getaway.

Back in Uncle Spence's driveway, I was pushing the plastic baggie to the bottom of my pocket when I felt the button blank and realized I was wearing the same shorts that I had worn to SAG on Monday. Somehow my unlucky charm had survived its trip through the wash. I pulled the blank from my pocket and stood rolling it around in my palm for a second. A metal garbage can sat in front of Uncle Spence's garage, only a few feet away. I took a step toward it, and then stopped. "I'm giving you one more chance," I warned out loud before I tucked the button blank into my pocket again.

THIRTEEN

THE URGE CAME over me the second I climbed back on my bike—like an itch that I was desperate to scratch—and suddenly I was flying past the Short Stop, on my way out to Fortune. *I won't stay long,* I told myself, pedaling faster. *Mom won't even miss me.*

I had just breezed past the first block when I heard a scraping sound coming from an alleyway up ahead. I slowed my feet on the pedals and coasted along, glancing down the passageways between the empty buildings on either side. My heart gave a little skip when I spotted the nose of a familiar green truck poking out from behind McNally and Sons.

I was so excited about seeing Garrett again that I forgot to be embarrassed as I parked my bike next to my old bench and hurried down the alley. Garrett was heaving a shovelful of shells into the bed of his pickup, and it wasn't until he looked up with a startled expression that I remembered all those faces around Hildy's dinner table staring at me in shocked silence.

"Hi," I said sheepishly. "Remember me?"

"Ren." Garrett lowered his shovel. "How could I forget? It seems you have a knack for turning up in unexpected places." He propped his big boot up on one side of the blade. "So what brings you out to Fortune on this fine Saturday?"

"I like to come here sometimes," I told him shyly. "It helps me think."

Garrett nodded as if that made perfect sense. I wanted him to keep talking, just so I could hear more of his English accent. "How's the labyrinth coming?" I asked.

"Good," he said. He fished a red rag out of his jeans pocket and mopped his sweaty brow. "I've got the design mostly laid out and after this load"—he nodded at the pile of shells punched with holes in the back of his truck—"I should have enough to see the project through."

"I'm surprised Hugh's not here helping you." I smiled sadly. I hadn't said Hugh's name out loud since I left the school, even though I had thought of him at least a dozen times in the last week. "How's he doing?"

Garrett's furry blond eyebrows drew together. "I haven't seen much of Hugh lately. I think the arrival of

Hildy's grandson might have knocked him off his perch a bit."

"Really? How come?"

"Well, he was used to having his run of the place, you know. Popping in and out of the museum and around corners at all hours. But that Tucker is as sharp as a fox, and I reckon he's put Hugh off by keeping too close an eye. And Mine mentioned there could have been some hurt feelings when Tucker gave Hugh a ribbing about those slippers he wears."

My mouth dropped open. "He made fun of Hugh's slippers?"

"I'm not exactly sure what was said, but it didn't go over very well."

Garrett had gone back to shoveling, and I stood in silence for a minute, seething inside as I pictured the scene at the school—the ugly smirk on Tucker's face as he teased Hugh about his Cubs slippers . . . and the pencil behind his ear . . . and his index cards. Why was I so surprised? I'd seen Mr. Baxter in action, the way he had needled Mayor Joy and Garrett at dinner. Like father like son.

I gave myself a shake and raised my voice over the clatter of shells echoing through the alley. "Can I help?"

"That would be lovely," Garrett shouted back. He stopped long enough to point at a rake propped against the edge of the tailgate. "You can climb up in the truck and drag the pile toward the back so I can get more in."

It was fun helping Garrett. Standing ankle-deep in shells, I almost felt like I was back in the old days—one of those kids Hildy had talked about who earned their keep in the button business. I figured the alley hadn't changed much from the way it looked a hundred years ago, as long as you didn't pay attention to the empty beer bottles and soda cans scattered along the edges. From my spot high in the truck, I could see through one of the dusty windows of the old factory. A neat stack of baby-blue boxes with lids still perched on a workbench as if they were waiting to be loaded with freshly cut buttons. And when I looked the other way, past a big metal shed that stood behind the factory, I could see a slice of the river and a flock of seagulls dipping and diving overhead.

After the truck was finally full, we sat on the tailgate to rest and Garrett passed me his battered jug of water once he had taken a long swig. "I don't have any germs." He grinned, wiping his mouth with the back of his hand. "Do you?"

"Not that I know of." I took a sloshing sip, and just like that it felt like we were friends. Garrett hadn't asked me a single question about the awful scene with my mom, and from what I could tell, he didn't really care.

"So you're from England?" I asked.

"Mostly," Garrett said with a mysterious smile.

"How'd you meet Hildy?"

"I was passing through Bellefield a few months ago and saw an advertisement for a handyman she had posted."

I sat up. "At the Short Stop?"

He nodded.

"That's how *I* met Hildy!"

"It's funny where life takes us, isn't it?" he mused. "If you had come to me ten years ago and said I'd pitch up in a place like this"—he waved his hand out at the shell-filled alleyway—"I'd never have believed you. But here we are."

"I heard you used to fix up old buildings in England." Just saying it sent a tingle through my veins. "That sounds so cool. Why would you want to leave that to come *here*?"

"Oh, the age-old story," Garrett said with a rueful laugh. "A girl."

I didn't want to be nosy, but Garrett must have sensed how curious I was. He gave me an amused glance. "Her name was Lenore and she came to England to study ancient turf labyrinths."

"Turf," I repeated. "What's that mean? They're made of grass?"

"That's right. You walk on paths of lawn with grooves cut in between. Lenore had come to visit a famous one in Lincolnshire that's been around since medieval times.

It's called Julian's Bower. I was working nearby, restoring an old church that had copies of the Bower design set into the stained-glass windows. Lenore came to see them and that's where we met." Garrett smiled faintly. "We hit it off, and the next thing I knew we were traveling together, visiting all the turf labyrinths the United Kingdom has to offer. I eventually followed her back here to the States."

"Then what happened?"

"Oh, things didn't work out between us," he said. "But I decided to stay on for a bit and explore."

Garrett glanced over at me again, chuckling at my perplexed expression. "I know it sounds daft, Ren, but I've spent my whole life drifting about. I like landing someplace and then learning the history of all the pieces I'm putting back together." He picked up a shell and weighed it in his big hand. "Look at this incredible thing, for instance. It's got one, two, five . . . *twelve* holes," he marveled, and passed it to me. I held it up to my eye like a spyglass, peering through one of the holes at a cloud and then a seagull breezing past. "Must have been a top-notch cutter who did that one. See how the holes are so close together with hardly any of the shell wasted?" Garrett shook his head. "Now there's a job I wouldn't envy."

"How come?"

"Oh, being a cutter was a wretched life," he said with

a grimace. He pushed himself off the tailgate and turned to face me, bending over like a hunchback. "Standing in the same position like this for hours, and the air was so thick with shell dust their noses and lungs would be clogged with the stuff from morning till night. And the machines?" Garrett made a *tsk*ing noise in his throat. "A *menace*. If you happened to lose your focus or look away from your saw, you could lose a finger in the blink of an eye. There were so many accidents that the owners of the bigger cutting shops would put finger jars on display to frighten their workers into being careful."

"Finger jars? What's a finger jar?"

"Why, just what it sounds like. A jar full of chopped-off fingers floating in formaldehyde."

I probably looked sick to my stomach.

Garrett laughed. "Forgive me, Ren. I didn't mean to keep nattering on about such gruesome stuff. Though it's fascinating, isn't it?"

"Yeah, but it's so much different than I pictured. I thought making buttons out of shells sounded so . . . peaceful."

"Well, it *was* peaceful in many ways," Garrett said as he screwed the lid back on his water jug. Then he paused. "Apart from the smell, of course."

"The smell?"

"Oh, this town must have stunk to high heaven on a hot summer's day. Not hard to imagine when you think of what was inside these tons of shells." Garrett swept his big hand up at the load in his truck. "According to the old-timers, you could smell Fortune coming from a mile away."

Garrett smacked his forehead with a loud laugh. "But hold on! I'm supposed to be telling you about the nice bits."

"Yes." I smiled. "What about the nice bits?"

"Well, let's see," he said, leaning back on the tailgate again and crossing his arms. "Lots of families used to set up camp down by the river in the summers and the kids got to sleep in tents and help their parents with the clamming." He cut his eyes over at me. "How am I doing?"

"Better," I said.

"Oh, and of course there were the pearls. Those were certainly the nicest bits of all."

I twisted around to face him. "Pearls?"

"Cleaning out these shells probably wasn't very pleasant, but some clammers made their fortune off the pearls they found inside."

"Really? I thought people only found pearls in oysters, from the ocean." I could feel my heart speeding up. Hildy's father had been a clammer.

"Nope. You can find pearls inside freshwater clams and mussels too. It wasn't too hard to find slugs," Garrett went on. "That's what they called the odd-shaped pearls, and those could fetch a good bit of money from the pearl buyers who came through town. But the real prize"—his low voice deepened even more, filling with suspense— "was a perfectly round pearl. Those were much rarer to find, and the clammers could practically name their own price."

I racked my brain trying to think of the exact words Hildy's brother, Tom, had written in his letter—something about how upset Pop would be when he discovered his missing box of treasure. Was that what Hildy had been looking for? Her father's pearls?

It had to be.

Garrett was looking at me funny. "Are you all right?" he asked. "Do you need another drink of water?"

"Oh, no," I said in a fluster. "I'm fine. I was just—" I glanced at my watch. Almost an hour had passed since I'd ridden my bike into Fortune. "I guess I better be getting home." I had been on the verge of asking Garrett straight out: *Did you know Hildy's looking for something in the school? Could it be her dad's long-lost stash of pearls?* But I was worried if I started talking I might not stop, and soon I'd be getting Hugh in trouble for spying and both of us in hot water for opening Hildy's safe. And what if Garrett told Hildy what I'd been talking about? She thought I was enough of a sneak already. I didn't want to make her impression of me even worse.

"Well, then . . ." Garrett's voice trailed off as he lodged the rake and shovel in the back of the truck. "Thanks so much for your help, Ren . . . and the company of course." He slammed the tailgate and slid his hands into his back jeans pockets with a wistful smile. "It can get sort of lonely around here."

"It was good to see you too," I said, turning to go. But then I stopped. "So you'll watch out for him, right? Hugh, I mean. To make sure Tucker isn't picking on him or anything?"

"I will." Garrett gave a firm nod. "And," he added, "I don't think anyone would mind if you paid a visit sometime to see for yourself."

"Really?" I squinted up at him through a blaze of sunlight that had come streaming into the alleyway. "Are you sure?"

It was too bright to see Garrett's expression, but I heard him say "I'm sure" in that rumbly voice of his, and a little swell of happiness rose up inside me as I waved goodbye.

Before I left Fortune, I stood straddling my bike in the middle of Front Street. My handlebars were pointed toward home, but I couldn't resist taking a long look over my shoulder at the lonely road that led to the turnoff for the school. I knew I'd find a way to go back. I just didn't know how, or when.

FOURTEEN

THE SECOND WEEK of SAG dragged by at a zombie's pace. Each day seemed worse than the last. On Thursday we presented our imaginary cities to the group, and I came close to shrieking at Arnold when it was our turn to do Moleville. We had decided that I'd be in charge of the introduction and describing our city's energy sources, but I couldn't get through two sentences without Arnold trying to take over. "And all the tunnels will have natural lighting," he interrupted for the third time. "We're bringing the sunlight in through fiber-optic cables."

When Stretch finally asked him to cut it out, Arnold crossed his arms and refused to say another word. So I had to do the whole last half by myself while he stood behind me making impatient noises in his throat like I was getting everything wrong.

Needless to say, I wasn't too excited that afternoon when Stretch told us to gather around so he could announce our next project. Never in a million years would I have guessed that the dreaded Summer Academy for the Gifted would offer the solution—the perfect excuse to convince Mom to let me go back to the school. But five minutes later, once I had heard the details of our new assignment, I was patting the button blank in my pocket and smiling to myself, thinking my luck had finally turned around.

Now I just needed to find the right time to present my case.

Unfortunately dinner wasn't an option, because Nora had talked Mom into letting Alain come over even though we were still grounded. There was no way I could bring up the school with Alain making moony eyes at my sister and Mom flitting back and forth offering him more Tater Tots and Sloppy Joe sandwiches.

It took another couple of hours for Alain to say *bonsoir*. I was brushing my teeth when Mom came into the bathroom carrying a basket of clean towels. By then I was too grumpy and tired to be very clever with my approach. I spit my mouthful of water into the sink and said, "I know I'm still supposed to be grounded and all, but I need you to make an exception for Saturday."

I watched my mother's face in the mirror. One eyebrow lifted. "Oh? And why's that?"

"It's an assignment for SAG," I said. I reached for my hairbrush, trying to act casual. "Stretch wants us all to pick a community service project and we're supposed to start volunteering this weekend."

"Okay," Mom said simply, as she set the laundry basket on the side of the tub.

I stopped with my brush in midair and turned around in surprise. "Really?"

She nodded. "I was already thinking two weeks was long enough for you and Nora to be grounded, and I won't be here on Saturday so I'm glad you'll have something to keep you busy."

"Why? Where are you going?"

Mom bent down to pick up a dirty washcloth. When she stood up, her face was flushed. "I'm going to do it, Ren," she declared. "I'm going to start my EMR training on Saturday."

"EMR training? What's that?"

"Emergency Medical Responder," Mom said excitedly. "Once I'm qualified, I can volunteer for the rescue squad."

"Ohhh." My voice swooped up, full of poison. "Now I get it. I'm not grounded anymore so you can go off with Rick and learn how to rescue people." I bumped against Mom's shoulder on my way out of the bathroom. Then I shoved past Nora, who had been lurking in the hall, probably eavesdropping on our whole conversation.

"I knew that's what you would think!" Mom cried as

she followed me to my bedroom. "But this isn't about Rick. Sure, he's the one who got me interested, but we won't be in class together. He already finished his training a long time ago."

I stood in front of my window, breathing hard while Mom kept arguing her case behind me. "Look, Ren. I've discovered something important these past few months. One of the main reasons I've been so unhappy lately is because of my job. My life at work is all about profits and losses and keeping track of money nonstop, and you know what? I miss being around *people*. These classes will give me the chance to explore something new and to do work that's . . . that's *alive and breathing*."

I realized I was still holding my brush. "So fine," I snapped as I began ripping the bristles through my tangled hair. I whirled around to face Mom. "Go off and do your rescue squad stuff with Rick. Do whatever you want! But just so you know, I've already picked my service project and it's the school in Fortune."

Mom's face went blank. "The school?"

"We're all supposed to pick a cause that we care about. Then we have to volunteer there at least three Saturdays. So I've decided to work at the school for my project."

Mom pulled her chin back in disbelief. "Honestly, Ren," she snorted. "You think I'm going to let you go back to that crazy place with all those squatters hanging around?"

"They're not squatters!" I shot back, even though I had no idea what a squatter was.

"And how do you think the school qualifies as a service project?" Mom went on. "That woman who owns it is running a business, not a charity."

"No, you don't understand. Hildy's making a museum in the gym and she needs help."

Mom threw up her hands. "A museum! What museum? You never mentioned anything about a museum before."

"That's because you were too mad to listen. You never even asked me about what it was like there." I sank onto my bed. My scalp hurt from brushing so hard. "It's a button museum and it could be really cool if—"

"A *button* museum?"

Suddenly, Nora appeared behind Mom in the doorway. She held her finger to her lips, signaling for me to pipe down. "Listen, Mom," she said as she came over to sit beside me. "You should let Ren go. You've got this EMR training that you're excited about, and you want Ren to support you, right? So you should do the same for her. I talked to the lady who owns that place, remember?"

Mom gave her a dry look. "Yes. Believe me, I remember."

"Well," Nora breezed on. "She sounded perfectly nice . . . and really responsible." Nora looked at me. "What's her name? Mrs. Baxter?"

I nodded with my mouth open, torn between wanting

to hug Nora or hit her. Judging by the offhand way she had said "EMR training," I could tell she wasn't hearing about Mom's rescue squad plans for the first time.

"That's the other thing!" Mom continued arguing. "You two tricked that woman. Outright lied to her." She swiveled to face me. "Do you really think she's going to welcome you back with open arms?"

"Well, maybe not with open arms, but—"

"Mom," Nora cut in. "Why don't you just give Mrs. Baxter a call and talk to her about it? I gave you her number, remember?"

Mom pressed her lips together tight. "Fine," she agreed after a heavy pause. "But I'm not promising anything." I blinked at Nora in amazement. All at once, I was ready to forgive her for everything—for her cute French boyfriend and her straight silky hair and her cell phone with its glittery case—even for being so chipper about Mom's plans to join the rescue squad with Rick. I'd have to stew over that later. But for now all I could think about was Saturday and whether Hildy would let me come back.

FIFTEEN

EVEN THOUGH MOM WAS RUNNING LATE for her rescue squad class, she slowed the car to a creep as we bumped into the driveway of the school.

"I don't know, Ren . . ." she said, eyeing everything suspiciously—the potholes, the rotten seesaws, and the rusted swing set. Mayor Joy was standing on a ladder at the far end of the parking lot with his head stuck under the hood of his eighteen-wheeler. I could see Wayne grazing in a patch of tall grass nearby.

"What's wrong?" I asked impatiently. We had it all planned. Mom was supposed to drop me and my bike off, then head back to town for her class. But now she was acting like she might change her mind.

Luckily Mayor Joy hopped down from his ladder and trotted over to Mom's window before she could put the car in reverse. "Mornin'," he said cheerily, crouching down so he could see us. "Can I help you?"

"Hi, Mayor Joy," I said, giving him an embarrassed little wave from the passenger seat.

His eyes lit up with recognition. "Oh, hey there! How you doing, young lady?" He glanced at Mom, who so far had remained stony behind her sunglasses. "Didn't think I'd ever see you two again."

"Yes, well," Mom answered uncomfortably. "My daughter's here for a service project. She wants to help in Mrs. Baxter's . . . button museum. I called yesterday and Mrs. Baxter said it would be fine, but now I'm wondering if I should go inside and make sure it's still all right for Ren to spend the day here."

I had been watching Wayne come ambling over as Mom was talking, and now he stretched out his neck, opened his grizzled muzzle wide, and let out a screechy hee-haw right behind the Mayor's ear.

My mother jumped in her seat and the Mayor whirled around. "Dang it, Wayne!" he cried. "Get on out of here!" He turned back to us, wincing. "My apologies, ladies. Wayne forgets his manners sometimes."

I was relieved when Mom laughed. "Well, I didn't know what to expect here this morning," she said, taking off her sunglasses, "but it certainly wasn't *that*." She checked her watch and gave Mayor Joy a searching look. I squirmed impatiently in my seat. How could she not trust a friendly old mayor who owned a pet donkey? "I *am* actually running a little late," Mom said nervously. "Do you think it's okay if I don't go in?"

"Perfectly fine," the Mayor assured her. "Hildy's going to be delighted to see your daughter. Believe me, she needs all the help she can get."

I jumped out of the car.

"I want you home by five, okay?" Mom reminded me through the window once she had popped the trunk and Mayor Joy had helped me lift my bike to the ground. I nodded over my shoulder as I parked my bike in the grass and turned to follow him up the steps. When I looked back, Mom was still there. "Wish me luck?" she called. Her voice hung in the air, high and thin, like a little girl's. I could feel how mean it was, but somehow, I couldn't make myself do it—wish my mother luck as she headed off to follow in Rick's footsteps. All I could do was lift my arm in a halfhearted wave.

Mayor Joy was holding the door open for me. "I bet Hildy's in the gym waiting for you," he said with a kind nod. "I've got to finish up a few things on my truck, but you go on in."

In the foyer, I glanced around, hoping I might catch a glimpse of Hugh hiding behind something or spying from the janitor's closet. But there was no trace of him, and when I got to the museum, I didn't see Hildy or Tucker either. I wandered along the edges of the gym, craning my neck to see over the piles of clutter and admiring the improvements that had been made in the last two weeks. The passageways had been widened. All the old button-company signs had been hung on the walls. And over on the other side of the gym, the button-cutting machines had been cleaned up and arranged in orderly rows for display.

"Hello?" I called timidly. No one answered. "Anyone home?" I hollered louder.

"Up here," someone croaked. I tipped my head back, scanning the balcony. After a minute, Hildy appeared at the far railing halfway down the gym. "The door to the stairs is over there," she called. "Next to the storage room."

The Mayor said Hildy would be "delighted" to see me, but she certainly didn't sound like it. *She's probably still mad,* I worried, as I picked my way up the staircase and stepped into the jumble of keepsakes that had been stuffed into the balcony.

I found Hildy sitting in a fold-out chair, thumbing through a pile of old photographs. Now it was obvious—something was definitely wrong. She wasn't wearing a single smudge of makeup and she barely looked in my direction as I wedged myself into the space beside her.

"Hi there," I said. There was a shoe box of pictures on a wooden trunk next to Hildy's chair. I scooted it aside so I could sit down. "Thanks for letting me come back." My mouth felt as dry as chalk as I scrambled for words to fill the silence. "I know you must have been really disappointed in me for lying to you, and I wanted to tell you again how sorry I am."

Hildy gave a little nod.

"Mom told you about the assignment for my summer camp, right?" I rambled on. "The community service thing? Well, everybody else at my camp is doing boring stuff like helping stock shelves at the food bank or clearing trails in the park, but I thought the museum would be way more interesting than those other projects."

The whole time I'd been talking, Hildy kept flipping through the pictures in her lap. She lingered over one—a black-and-white photo of a young boy and a man, standing on the deck of a boat heaped with shells—then finally lifted her tired gaze. Without her eyebrows and lipstick painted on, her face looked pale and stripped, like a tree branch without its bark. "Oh, honey," she said. "I appreciate the apology and the fact that you wanted to come back and help. But to be honest, I don't know if this foolishness of mine is really worth your time."

"What do you mean? Your museum isn't foolish."

Hildy shook her head. "I'm starting to think maybe Jack's right. Maybe I'm just wallowing in the past, and nobody will care one bit about what life on the river was like in the old days or a piddly little thing like how buttons used to be made."

Hildy had a denim apron tied over her outfit, and she

reached down into its wide front pocket. "And look at this," she said, pulling out a stack of envelopes. "This is what I find waiting for me when I go to the mailbox every morning." She dropped the envelopes on top of the photos in her lap. "Bills, bills, and more bills." Shifting in her chair, she winced as if she could feel her bones grinding in their sockets. "The truth is I don't think my bank account's big enough to see this thing through. Real museums—they've got display cases and proper restrooms . . . those ramps for handicapped people. All that equipment costs a lot of money. Money I don't have at the moment."

A whisper had started in my head like the steady tick-tick of a time bomb ready to explode—*the treasure, the treasure, what about the missing treasure?* But of course I couldn't tell Hildy that I had discovered her secret, not when I had barely finished apologizing for all the other stuff I had done. "What about your son?" I asked instead. "Can't you talk him into lending you some money?"

"Puh." Hildy blew out a disgusted puff of air. "Like I said, Jack thinks I've gone senile. He'd like nothing better than for me to give up and move out of this place, spend the rest of my days in an old folks' home."

Poor Hildy. Not only was she low on money, but her son didn't trust her to run the museum, much less a rooming house. I was sure the awful scene Mom and I had made in the cafetorium had made it even more difficult for her to prove her case.

I had to make it up to her. "Hildy," I burst out. "I've got to tell you something. You're probably going to be really mad."

"Oh, mercy," she breathed, straightening her glasses on her nose. "What is it?"

"Remember that day I spent here? Before my mom came to get me?"

She nodded warily.

"Well—" I gulped. "When I was exploring with Hugh, I kept seeing those chalkboards with the word *no* written on them. I started asking questions and Hugh told me that *you* were the one who writes on the boards, not Garrett, and Hugh says you've been looking for something."

Hildy's jaw—every part of her—stiffened. I blinked my eyes shut, and when I opened them again, I opened my mouth too and didn't stop talking until the whole story was out. "I'm really sorry, Hildy," I said, when I had finished telling the worst parts. "I know it sounds sneaky and awful, breaking into your safe like that, but I swear we were never going to take anything. Hugh just wanted to look inside to see if we could figure out what you'd been searching for, and then when we found that letter from your brother, it was so . . . I don't know, *mysterious* . . . that . . . well, I guess we couldn't stop ourselves from reading it." I clamped my teeth down on my bottom lip and braced for what was coming next.

But nothing that I had been expecting to happen happened. Hildy didn't yell or tell me to get out or give me a long lecture. Instead she started to chuckle. It started deep in her throat, and soon her skinny shoulders were shaking. I stared at her in bewilderment, my mouth hovering on the edge of a smile.

Hildy took off her glasses and wiped her eyes with the bottom corner of her apron. "Doesn't that beat all?" she said. "That little stinker. How'd he find the combination? I'd have never known it was in that drawer if the last principal hadn't come by for a visit and pointed it out to me."

"So you're not mad?" I asked in disbelief.

Hildy pulled herself up disapprovingly. "Oh, don't get me wrong," she said. "I think you kids were way out of line to open that safe without permission and then read a letter that wasn't addressed to you. But"—she lifted her shoulders in a resigned shrug—"I suppose what's done is done, and at least you had the courage to own up to what you did."

"And, Hildy, now that you know the truth, we can help you," I told her. "Hugh and I. We can help you find your missing treasure, and then maybe you could sell it and use the money to finish the museum." I leaned forward, my voice rising with excitement. "It's pearls, isn't it?"

"Shhhhh." Hildy held her finger against her lips, cocking her head to listen. "Tucker might be down there," she rasped, "and I don't want him to hear any of this."

"How come?"

Hildy listened a few seconds longer, and then murmured, "Because he might tell his father. And Jack already thinks I'm senile enough as it is. He's heard me talk about the missing pearls for years, but he doesn't want to hear about it anymore. He hates to think I might have bought this place just because I think they're still hidden here."

I glanced uneasily over my shoulder. "Where *is* Tucker, by the way?"

"He's sorting through my shell collection today and taking the ones we don't want out to Garrett. So he's probably out back at the labyrinth."

"So what does your son think happened to the pearls?"

"Oh, he has all sorts of theories. He thinks maybe one of the students stumbled across them, or maybe my father found Tom's hiding place after all. But his favorite theory is that Mr. Bonnycastle took them."

"What? Wasn't Mr. Bonnycastle your brother's good friend?"

"Sure was. But Jack likes to remind me that greed does funny things to people. Tom's letter didn't show up at school until a few months after he'd been killed. I'm not sure why it took so long to arrive. But by the time it did, Bonny had moved on, supposedly to a teaching job out east somewhere. Jack's convinced that Tom must have accidentally let something slip before he left for basic training and that Bonny had figured out where the pearls were hidden, then skipped town as soon as he found them."

"How'd you get the letter then? If Bonny was already gone?"

"The school secretary delivered it to me. After graduation I worked in a little secondhand shop in town. Thank heavens she brought it there instead of dropping it off at the house with Pop. He would have opened it for sure."

"So you never got to talk to Mr. Bonnycastle and ask him what he was doing that day when Tom came to the school to say goodbye?"

Hildy shook her head sadly. "I tried for years to track him down. There were no computers or Internet back then, remember, so I put advertisements in the big city newspapers. Talked to everyone who had known him." She scratched at her forehead in concentration, tugged her wig back into place, and then went on. "But Bonny had always been a bit of a mystery."

"What do *you* think? Do you think Mr. Bonnycastle took the pearls?"

"No, I don't," she replied firmly. "All the kids here used to adore Bonny. He was such a sweet young man . . . not much older than Tom, but he had a heart condition so they wouldn't let him join the service. He'd stride up and down the aisles, reading out loud and using different voices for the characters in his favorite books. He did a wonderful Sir Lancelot . . . and King Lear." Hildy smiled to herself, remembering. "And you should have seen us shiver when he read Edgar Allan Poe stories on Halloween. That old skull you discovered would always make an appearance. And at Christmas he played carols for the pageant. He was quite a piano player, that Bonny, in addition to being a good artist. He used to spend hours in the music room tinkling away." Hildy had crossed her arms stubbornly. "No sir," she declared. "I don't think there was a shifty bone in that man's body. And my brother, he was a good judge of character. He'd never have chosen a friend who would turn on him like that."

"So that means we should keep looking," I insisted, thumping my fist on my knee. I knew I was supposed to be there to help in the museum, but weren't the pearls more important right now? Especially with Hildy on the verge of giving up? "We should start over again and make sure you didn't miss anything. What did the box look like?"

"It was plain. Made out of old pine wood. About this big." Hildy held her hands half a foot apart. "If you saw it, you'd never guess there was a fortune inside. But heavens, Ren," she said, sighing. "I already searched this whole place from top to bottom. And I must have read my brother's letter more than a hundred times looking for clues. Who knows what Bonny was doing that day my brother came to say goodbye. He could've been anywhere. Bonny was like Garrett—good at fixing things—so Mr. Harper had him traipsing all over the school with his tool kit. He was the only one who could keep the old boiler in the basement going—"

Down below there was a faint clank of metal. Hildy sat up straight as another clang, much louder, echoed through the gym. "Tucker's back," she said, gathering up the bills in her lap and pushing them back in her apron pocket. "Let's go on down and see what he's up to."

Before I helped Hildy to her feet, she asked me to set her stack of photographs back in the shoe box on the trunk—but not before she picked off the top one, of the man and the boy on the boat. "Tom and my father," she told me, giving the picture one last look before she tucked it into her apron pocket along with the bills. "During happier times."

I had at least a dozen more questions to ask. What had caused all the bitterness with her dad? And would she let Hugh and me hunt for the pearls too? *And what about the museum?* I wondered as I shuffled along the railing behind Hildy, looking down on all those memories heaped across the gym. Was she really ready to let go of all that?

Hildy cut my wondering short as we reached the top of

the stairs. "Remember now," she said, turning and putting her finger to her lips again. "Mum's the word."

Mum's the word. Her warning rang a bell. Then it hit me. Those were the same instructions Tom had written in his last letter to Hildy.

SIXTEEN

TUCKER TRIED TO ACT like he wasn't the least bit interested to see me. "Oh, hey," was all he said when Hildy reintroduced us. But then I noticed his ears had turned red, and when Hildy started quizzing him about his progress that morning, he had a little trouble keeping up his cool-guy routine.

With her hands on her hips, Hildy stood looking over the buckets filled with shells that were lined up outside the storage room. The shells were all shapes and sizes and they didn't have any holes cut through. "So are you getting the hang of telling them apart?" Hildy asked Tucker. "Are you being sure to check that shell guide I gave you?"

Tucker shrugged. "I don't really need to use the book anymore."

Hildy bent down with a grunt and plucked a long black shell from the top of the nearest bucket. "What's this one?" she asked, holding it out to Tucker.

He gnawed the corner of his bottom lip as he came over to take it. "That's a . . . wait, let me think." He turned the shell over and over in his hands. After what I had heard about Tucker making fun of Hugh's slippers, I enjoyed seeing him squirm.

"Is it a spectacle-case?" he finally guessed.

"Nope." Hildy smiled. "Black sandshell. But that's an honest mistake. Those two look a lot alike. What about this one?" She held up a thick brown shell with knobs running down the center.

"A sheepnose!" Tucker blurted out.

Hildy punched the air with delight. "Bingo!" she cried.

But Tucker, obviously embarrassed by his little flash of excitement, had already returned his face to its usual blank expression. "Here, I'll take it," he said, as he reached for Hildy's shell. He stepped over to a worktable against the wall. There were a dozen or so labeled shoe boxes lined up on top and he dropped the black shell into one of the boxes and then walked farther down the row and dropped the sheepnose into another.

I followed Hildy over to take a closer look and read the names on the labels. They were a funny assortment—fat mucket . . . fawnsfoot . . . monkeyface . . . pigtoe . . . pistol-grip . . . purple wartyback. I peered into the box labeled

"Butterfly" and picked up the single shell that sat inside. It was delicate and yellow with a pattern of darker markings fanning out from the narrow end, just like a butterfly's wing.

After she had finished inspecting the shoe boxes, Hildy turned to Tucker appreciatively. "You'll be an expert by the time this is done, honey, and we'll have one of the best shell collections in the whole state."

"Where'd you get all these?" I asked Hildy.

"Oh, here and there. My dad collected them back in his clamming days and different folks have brought me theirs over the years. A lot of these species weren't any good for button-making of course, but the old-timers knew they were disappearing fast from the Mississippi. They liked keeping a few so they wouldn't forget what they looked like." Hildy let out a dry laugh. "Whenever old geezers from Fortune would kick the bucket, I'd get their bucket of shells." I glanced over to see if Tucker had cracked a smile yet, but he wasn't even listening.

"So, Ren," she said, "if you're ready to get started on that service project of yours, you can give Tucker a hand going through the rest of these shells. It'll go a lot faster with the two of you working together. Whenever you're not sure of something, just ask Tucker. He can show you the ropes."

"Okay," I said weakly.

Tucker didn't seem any happier about the situation

than I did. "Wait, Hildy," he called as she started to shuffle off. "Where are you going?"

"Oh, I haven't been sleeping too well lately," she said vaguely. "I'm ready for a catnap. I'll be back in an hour or so." After Hildy had gone, Tucker and I didn't say anything for a few minutes. I stood at the table flipping through the shell guide. Most of the shells in the pictures looked exactly alike—brown and oval. How was I supposed to tell the difference?

I glanced over my shoulder. Tucker had dragged one of the buckets closer to the wheelbarrow and was picking through the shells on top. Every once in a while, the clang of a shell on metal rang out through the quiet gym. I took a deep breath and turned around. "Can you show me what I'm supposed to be doing here?"

Tucker lazily bumped his sneaker against the side of the bucket at his feet. "You can go through the rest of these if you want and get rid of all the deertoes and hickorynuts. We've already got too many of those." He fished two shells out of his pail and held them out for me to see. Thankfully, they looked nothing alike. The hickorynut was golden colored, rounded with dark ridges, and the deertoe actually looked like a small hoof—glossy black with a pointed edge.

I nodded and knelt down. "So," I piped up, hurrying to start a conversation before the awkward silence had time to settle in again. "How do you like it here so far?"

Tucker gave me a "what do you think?" look. He sauntered over to a knee-high metal can full of shells and hoisted it up. "Worst . . . summer . . . ever," he grunted out as he stiff-legged the heavy can closer to the wheelbarrow. He banged it down on the floor with a big huff of air.

"Oh, it can't be *that* bad."

Tucker cut his eyes at me underneath his bangs. "Oh, yeah? How'd you like to be stuck for eight weeks where there's no Internet, no air-conditioning, nobody to talk to under the age of fifty—"

I kept picking through my shells. "Garrett and Mine are nowhere near that old. And they both seem really nice to me."

"Yeah, maybe," Tucker admitted. "But that Mine? She can't cook worth squat."

I decided to let that one slide. "Well, what about Hugh?" I fished. I'd been itching to bring him up ever since Hildy left. "He's under fifty."

"Hugh?" Tucker snorted. "That kid's one of the reasons I can't wait to get out of here. Gives me the creeps."

I could feel myself bristling. "How can he give you the creeps? He's only eight."

"When I first got here, every time I turned around he was hiding behind some corner watching me with those spooky Martian eyes of his." Tucker flipped back his bangs and popped his eyes open wide like some psycho from a horror movie. "I finally got tired of it, him always sneaking up on me, so I made sure it wouldn't happen again."

"What do you mean?" I asked. "What'd you do?"

Tucker didn't seem to notice how icy my voice had turned. He strolled over to the worktable. "I decided to show him what it feels like," he said as he plunked a keeper shell into one of the boxes. "He likes hanging out in the old chemistry lab, so one afternoon I hid in the closet and waited for him, and, well"—Tucker's shoulders twitched with a snide laugh—"let's just say I don't think Hugh will be spying on me again anytime soon."

I glared at Tucker's back. "You must have really scared him, which is pretty rude considering he was only spying because he's bored and doesn't have any friends to play with around here. You should try getting to know him. He's really smart."

Tucker turned to face me, still looking amused. "Huh. You could have fooled me. He sure messed things up at the labyrinth this morning."

"What are you talking about?"

"Garrett tried to stop him, but it was too late." One corner of Tucker's mouth lifted in a slow smile. "Hugh had already left his mark."

I stood up, wiping my hands on my shorts. Trying to get Tucker to give a straight answer was like talking to one of those Magic 8 Balls. *Reply hazy, try again.*

"Where's Hugh now?" I demanded. "Is he still out at the labyrinth?"

"Probably not," Tucker said with a half shrug. "Once Garrett yelled at him, he dropped his weapon and ran."

Weapon?

"Whatever," I snapped as I marched past the shell buckets. "I'm going to go check on Hugh. I'm sure you'll do just fine here without me for a while."

SEVENTEEN

MINE STARTLED ME with a big hug when she answered the door to the library. "Ren! You're back!" she crooned as I blinked into the soft gauze of her top, breathing in her cinnamon-and-burnt-toast smell. She pulled away. "Hildy said you were coming to help in the museum." She lowered her voice, still gripping my shoulders. "I'm so glad. Hugh could use a buddy right now . . . other than his mom." She gave me a little push in the direction of the card catalog. "Go on back. He'll be really happy to see you."

When I peeked through the tie-dyed curtains that hung around Hugh's bottom bunk, he was sitting in the corner, hugging a pillow to his chest. I pushed the curtains apart and crawled into the open space at the end. It was warm and shadowy in there, like an animal's den. "How's it going?" I asked carefully, once I had crisscrossed my legs in front of me and pulled the curtains closed. Even in the shadows, I could see Hugh had been crying. His face was puffy and his lashes were clumped with tears. And worst of all, he was wearing socks and sneakers instead of his Cubs slippers.

"I don't like it here anymore," he said. "I wish we could move back to Chicago."

"It's because of Tucker, isn't it? Has he been picking on you?"

It took me a minute to follow the muffled rush of words that drifted out from behind Hugh's pillow. "—Hildy told Mine we'd have all the breathing room we needed. The first day we got here I counted up the rooms because it sounded really good—all that space for breathing. There's thirty-two, if you don't count closets, but that's not enough space if someone's watching you all the time. How am I supposed to breathe when someone's watching me all the time?"

"Who's watching you all the time? You mean Tucker?"

Hugh poked his head up a little ways and nodded, his eyes glistening.

I waited for a few seconds before I answered. "You know it's kind of funny. Tucker said the same thing about you. He said you're driving him crazy the way you keep hiding behind corners spying on him."

Hugh shook his head in aggravation. "I only spy on

people because I'm curious. But Tucker does it to be mean." He finally let go of his pillow and gave it a punch.

I stared at Hugh's neck. "What's that?" I gasped. His throat was smeared with red and his T-shirt was covered in crimson splatters. "Are you bleeding?"

Hugh scrubbed his hand miserably back and forth across his neck. "No. It's only spray paint, but I can't get it off."

"Spray paint? Who sprayed you? Was it Tucker?"

"No, I did it. I sprayed myself . . . and a lot of other stuff too."

"Wait, I don't understand. Why would you do that?"

"It was an accident." Hugh's face began to crumple again and he swiped a fist across his eyes. "This morning Garrett scratched out paths for the labyrinth in the dirt on the baseball field and he said we had to outline the marks in spray paint in case it rained."

"Okay. Then what?"

"Then Garrett said I could do some of the painting, but the button on my spray can got stuck right when Tucker came out there with his wheelbarrow, and he kept watching me like he always does. I didn't want to look dumb and ask Garrett for help, so I checked the little hole in the button to see if it was clogged and I pushed it one more time and all of a sudden it went off . . . and it wouldn't stop."

"So paint went everywhere?" I asked, trying to hide the croak of laughter in my voice.

He nodded glumly. "I sprayed a bunch of Garrett's shells and all over the path, and I kind of . . ."

"You kind of what?"

"I kind of sprayed Garrett."

That did it. I couldn't hold it in anymore. "I'm sorry, Hugh." I cackled helplessly. "But it reminds me of a skunk, the way you're telling the story. Did Garrett run away or did he just stand there and get sprayed more?"

Hugh had started to giggle too. "No, he ran away . . . just like . . . just like I was a stinky skunk!" Hugh flopped back on the bed. But after a few seconds, his giggles petered out and he popped up again like a sad jack-in-the-box. "I didn't get to say I was sorry. I just dropped the can and ran inside. Now Garrett's going to hate me. I ruined his labyrinth."

"Of course he's not going to hate you," I assured him. "And you didn't ruin anything. It's only paint, and Garrett's got tons of shells. Besides . . ." I smiled mysteriously. "We've got more important things to worry about."

Hugh's fierce eyebrows stayed puckered together. "Like what?"

"Like finding Hildy's treasure."

His face lit up. "What do you mean?"

"I told Hildy everything this morning—all about us opening her safe. She wasn't nearly as mad as I thought she'd be, and now I know what's in the box she's looking for."

"You do?" Hugh bounced up and down on the mattress. "*What?* What is it?"

"*Pearls,*" I said in a thrilled whisper.

"Pearls?" Hugh had grown still again. "Mine has a necklace with a pearl in it . . . So Hildy just came right out and told you her secret?"

"Not exactly. I had already figured it out before I talked to her. I ran into Garrett last weekend when I was riding my bike through Fortune and I helped him shovel shells for a while. He told me about how some of the clammers used to get rich off the pearls they found when they cleaned out their shells, and all of a sudden I knew."

"Why didn't Garrett ever tell *me* that?" Hugh asked.

I shrugged. "The subject never came up, I guess. I talked my mom into letting me come back here on weekends so I can help in the museum, but whenever I can, I'm going to sneak out so we can go hunt for the pearls."

"Why do we have to sneak if Hildy knows everything?"

"Because Hildy doesn't want Tucker to find out what we're doing."

Hugh bounced a little more. "How come?"

"She's afraid he'll tell his dad, and then Mr. Baxter will think she's crazy and try to put her in a nursing home." I fixed Hugh with a hard look. "So we've got to keep this a secret, okay?"

"I'm good at keeping secrets." He made a "zip your lip" sign.

"And we need to come up with a search plan. A systematic one."

"Want me to go get my index cards?" Hugh asked eagerly.

"Not right now. I have to get back to the gym to help Tucker." I rolled my eyes. "But I'm hoping Mom will let me come tomorrow too."

Hugh's face clouded over. "Tomorrow?" he whined. "What am I supposed to do till then?"

"Go apologize to Garrett," I ordered, and wagged my finger at the blaze of red on his throat. "And see if he's figured out how to get that skunk spray off."

When we climbed out of Hugh's bunk-bed cave, I found myself surveying all the nooks and crannies in the cozy back half of the library. The pearls could be anywhere. "How many rooms did you say are in this place?" I whispered.

"Thirty-two."

Not counting closets, I remembered, feeling more overwhelmed by the minute. But I forced a cheerful note into my voice as I said goodbye to Hugh. "If the pearls are here, we'll find them," I promised.

• • • • •

Tucker was on the defensive when I got back to the gym. "So what'd Hugh say about me? I bet he said the spray-paint thing was all my fault, right?"

I knelt down next to my bucket of shells again. "No," I answered. "But he says you make him nervous. He thinks you're looking over his shoulder all the time."

"*Me?* He's the one who goes around taking notes on people."

"I have an idea," I flung out. "Why don't you just try ignoring him and mind your own business?"

I hadn't meant to sound so witchy. But the damage was done. Tucker stopped talking to me after that, and we spent the rest of the day sorting shells in silence.

• • • • •

That evening Rick stopped by on his walk with Chauncey, and now he and Mom were standing in the front yard talking. As I stood in the living room peeking around the drapes, I could see my mother smiling and motioning excitedly. Snatches of her conversation drifted through the window screens. ". . . Everyone's so friendly . . . I can't wait till we get to the hard-core stuff like broken bones and heart attacks . . ."

I had barely asked Mom about her first day of training when I got home from Fortune. I didn't need to. It was obvious how much she loved it from the way she was

bustling around the kitchen getting dinner ready, singing along with the oldies station on the radio, and pelting
me with questions about Hildy's museum. I could see how
hard she was trying to fix things between us, but my
heart felt too small and shrunken to tell her more than
the bare minimum. She finally gave up after dinner and
went outside to water the flower boxes on the porch, and
that's when Rick happened to come strolling by.

After I watched him shoo a mosquito away from my
mother's face and throw his head back and laugh at something she said, I'd had enough. I charged over to flip the
porch lights on even though a slice of bright orange sun
was still glowing above the rooftops across the street.
Rick and Mom glanced up, startled, when I yanked the
front door open.

"Hey there, Ren," Rick said warily. "How's it goin'?"

"Fine," I told him. I marched to the edge of the top
step. Poor Chauncey was whimpering, waiting for me to
come down and greet him properly, but I stayed firmly
rooted to my perch. "Mom, I forgot to ask you if I can go
back to help in the museum tomorrow. Can I?"

"Two days in a row?" Mom asked. "And we've got
church in the morning. Isn't volunteering at the school
once a week enough?"

"Hildy needs all the extra help she can get. I could go
right after church," I said, firing my words out like bul-
lets. "Nora can take me. Or I can ride my bike."

Mom slapped at a mosquito. "Oh, all right," she said in a weary voice. "You can go."

"Thank you," I answered primly. Then I sat myself down on the top step and waited until Rick gave up and said good night.

EIGHTEEN

HUGH WAS ON THE FRONT STEPS of the school when I rattled up on my bike on Sunday afternoon. "I didn't think you were coming," he said as he trotted out on the walkway to greet me. An old army canteen swung from a strap around his neck.

I lurched off my bike and pushed the kickstand down. "Can I have a drink of that?" I motioned to Hugh's canteen. It had been blazing hot on the way over, with heat waves shimmering up from the pavement and crickets batting against my legs. I hadn't even bothered asking Mom or Nora for a ride. As soon as we got home from church, Mom had buried her nose in her first responder textbook and Nora had shut herself in her room to call Alain.

"You got here just in time," Hugh told me as I swallowed a few gulps of his lukewarm water. "Mine says it's too hot to do anything so she's taking a nap. And Hildy took Tucker to lunch and a movie in Bellefield."

I handed his canteen back and checked the parking lot. The Mayor's truck was gone. "Where're Garrett and the sisters?"

"The sisters are in their room and Garrett's out back."

"I see you got the paint off," I said as Hugh looped the canteen strap over his neck again. "Garrett must have forgiven you."

"Yeah, he even let me help him spray the last section of the path this morning. Then I told him I had to go because you were coming over. But I didn't say anything about the pearls," he added quickly.

"Great. So how long do you think we've got before Mine wakes up and starts looking for you?"

"Maybe an hour or two. She's got both our fans pointed on her."

Hugh's voice grew hushed when we stepped inside the foyer. "So where do we start?" he asked.

Good question. I'd been thinking about it all night. It didn't make sense to start searching the school completely from scratch—top to bottom, room to room. Combing through thirty-two rooms plus closets would take forever, and Tucker would start getting suspicious if I sneaked out of the museum too often for our investigations. We had to use every minute wisely.

I slid my backpack off my shoulders. "Remember in Tom's letter—how he wrote that Bonny was the one who had given him the idea for the hiding place? He said something like 'there it was, right under Bonny's nose.' Obviously Mr. Bonnycastle is the key to the mystery. So I think we should start with all of his old hangouts." I reached into the front pocket of my backpack and pulled out an index card with a flourish.

Hugh's face brightened. "Hey, you copied me."

"Yep. I decided to try your approach and write down all the stuff Hildy told me about Mr. Bonnycastle yesterday. Turns out she gave me some good clues for deciding where we should look first." I wagged the card in the air. "So this is the list I came up with."

Hugh plucked the card out of my hand and read what I had written. His expression turned squeamish. "You want to start with the boiler room?"

I nodded. "Hildy said Bonny was good at fixing things and supposedly he was the only one who knew how to keep the boiler running. So maybe he was working on it when Tom came to see him that day. Makes sense, right? The basement would be the perfect place for hiding a box of pearls."

"But Hildy was down there an awful long time. Don't you think she would've found the box already if Tom had hidden it there?"

"I bet she missed a bunch of spots. Hildy's pretty spry,

but she can't exactly get down on her hands and knees or squeeze into tight places like we can." I reached in my backpack again and brought out a flashlight for Hugh and then one for me. Hugh solemnly clicked his on and off to see if it was working. I clicked mine on too and waved the beam over the walls of the entrance hall, letting it land on the old school banner that hung above the trophy case. "That's what we are, Hugh," I said. "Fortune Hunters."

"Fortune Hunters," he repeated, testing the name under his breath. His mouth twitched up in a smile.

• • • • •

Even in the daytime, the school's basement was much creepier than I had imagined it would be. It felt like a dungeon. The floor joists over our heads were shrouded in spiderwebs and the dank smell that I had caught whiffs of upstairs seemed to ooze from every crevice in the cellar's clammy stone walls. Hugh and I stood for a minute at the bottom of the stairs, getting our bearings and aiming our flashlights into the darkest corners. There was no other light besides a bare bulb that hung down between the beams at the center of the main room. The furnace sat like a huge sleeping monster just beyond the bulb's pale glow.

"What's back there?" I whispered, nodding toward a narrow passageway on the other side of the boiler.

I could almost see Hugh gulp. "More rooms," he said.

"But I'm not too sure what's in them. I was worried Hildy would catch me if I followed her too close down here so I didn't go much past that doorway."

We started with the furnace, sticking together as we peered into the hidden spaces behind the soot-covered valves and rusted pipes. Then I turned toward the cluttered rows of storage shelves that stretched along the entire length of the opposite wall. "We've got to split up a little so we can cover more ground," I told Hugh. "You take that end and I'll take the other."

I should have remembered to bring work gloves along with the flashlights. The shelves were sprinkled with mouse poop, and it was disgusting picking through the jumble of dusty paint cans, grimy rags, and broken tools, not knowing exactly what my hand might land on next.

"Hugh, maybe this isn't such a good plan after all," I said after another five minutes of searching. I plucked a stray cobweb off my T-shirt and scraped my fingers through my ponytail, feeling for more. "It's like finding a needle in a haystack."

"What?" Hugh squeaked. "We just got started. Come on." His canteen clunked against his side as he grabbed my hand and began dragging me toward the far reaches of the basement. "You're the one who said we're the Fortune Hunters, remember?"

"Me and my bright ideas," I muttered.

We both stopped at the entrance to the back passageway. There was a light switch mounted on the wall nearby, but when I flipped it up and down nothing happened.

"Fortune Hunters," Hugh chanted, pointing his flashlight into the gloom. We huddled closer and shuffled forward.

"See?" Hugh chirped once we had edged into the first room along the narrow corridor. "This isn't so bad." The floor was piled with old textbooks. We poked around for a while, cracking open a few covers that had grown soft and moldy with age.

The next room seemed pretty harmless too—even empty. But then my light skimmed across a grim face in the corner and I snatched at Hugh's arm.

"What's wrong?" he yelped.

"Over there!"

Hugh swung his flashlight around, and I uncurled my fingers from his skinny bicep. "Oh," I croaked, letting out a sheepish laugh. "Sorry about that." A row of presidents—George Washington, Thomas Jefferson, and Abraham Lincoln—stared back at us. Their forgotten portraits sat on a shelf, propped against the wall in cracked and dusty frames. "Poor guys," I said. "I bet they never thought they'd end up in a place like this."

I felt a little bolder as we stepped into the passageway again. We only had one more room to go. This time I went in first and breathed a sigh of thanks when I tried the switch by the door and the light flickered on, revealing a room full of cardboard boxes. Hugh pushed past me and began lifting the sagging lids. "Cool!" he cried. The boxes were stuffed with retired uniforms—football jerseys in faded green and gold, old-fashioned one-piece gym suits, moth-eaten cheerleader sweaters. Hugh dug deep into a box of marching-band uniforms and pulled out a tall fuzzy hat. I couldn't help snickering when he put it on and started high-stepping around the edges of the room. The hat was way too big for him and it had a droopy green plume that flopped around like a dying bird. But in the next instant, my laugh turned into a shriek.

Hugh wheeled around and his hat banged to the floor. "What now?"

I stabbed my finger at the doorway. "I saw something move out there."

"Like what?"

"I don't know," I whimpered. "Who cares? Let's get out of here."

This time Hugh didn't try to argue. I snapped off the switch by the door and we both bolted for the stairs. But as we scurried along the passageway, it happened again. I jerked back in terror and let out another screech.

"Stop doing that!" Hugh yelled as he stumbled into me, losing his grip on his flashlight.

"I can't!" I yelled back. "Something brushed against my leg!"

Hugh was bending down, scrabbling for his light. "Wait for me!" he cried as I took off running. "Ren! Wait!"

Halfway across the boiler room, I forced myself to stop and look over my shoulder. *Why wasn't he coming?* "Hugh?" I called in a trembling voice.

"Shhhh," I heard him say. I backtracked a few steps and found Hugh frozen in the passageway. He had trained his light on some paint cans that were stacked at the end of the corridor outside the uniform room. I stared at the circle of light on the stone wall, clenching every muscle. It took my last shred of willpower to keep from screaming again when a pair of glowing gold eyes appeared.

Hugh started to giggle. "It's Flam!"

"Jeez," I gasped, my shoulders slumping with relief as the creature slunk into view.

"I should have known," Hugh said. "Whenever they get loose, they sneak down here to hunt mice."

Flam sat coolly regarding us. "How do you know which one's which?" I asked.

"Flam's got more spots than Flim."

"Hey," I whispered. "Do you think we can catch him? Hildy said Mr. Bonnycastle loved playing the piano, so the music room's next on my list. If we bring Flam back, maybe the sisters will invite us in and we can take a look around."

"I don't know," Hugh said. "Those cats aren't very friendly. Whenever I try to pet them, they run away."

I eyed Flam's tail flicking back and forth. "We're going to need some bait. Have you got any tuna fish upstairs? Or what about a bowl of milk?"

While Hugh went sprinting off to the kitchen, I stood on the stairs guarding the escape route. It took Hugh forever to come back. I flung my hands up in exasperation when I saw what he was carrying—a dish full of Lucky Charms smeared with peanut butter.

"Well, sorr-eeee," Hugh huffed. "I couldn't get the can opener to work, and milk's hard to carry without spilling. Besides, milk's boring. If I were a cat, this is what I'd want."

Hugh sneaked down to set the plate on the floor, a few feet from the stairs. Then we sat on the bottom step to wait. "Here, kitty, kitty, kitty," I trilled softly. We'd never owned any cats, so I had no idea how to go about catching one. But I was pretty sure dry cereal—even "magically delicious" cereal—wasn't the answer.

"Meow," Hugh called in a screechy voice. "Me-owww." I choked back a laugh. It was the worst impression of a cat I had ever heard. But incredibly, seconds later, Flam came padding around the corner of the furnace.

"Don't . . . move," Hugh ordered under his breath, and soon the cat was happily crouched over the plate, lapping at the lumps of peanut butter.

"What do we do now?" I whispered.

Hugh didn't answer. He rose from the steps in slow motion and edged closer and closer. Then, just when I thought Flam might dart away, he swooped down and snatched the cat up in his arms. "Hugh!" I cried as I jumped to my feet. "That was amazing!"

Flam had taken the bait. Now we'd have to see if the sisters would too.

NINETEEN

FLAM WAS HISSING MAD by the time Colette finally opened the door to the old music room. "Oh, Flam," she gushed. "Mind your manners. Is that any way to thank Hugh for bringing you home?" Like before when I had stood at the sisters' threshold, a gust of flowery smells swept into the hallway as Colette cracked the door wider and reached for her pet. "Here I'll take him—"

But Hugh kept squeezing Flam's grumpy face into the crook of his neck. He stood on his tiptoes, trying to see past Colette. "Are you making soap today?" he asked. "Can Ren and I come in and watch? Ren's always wanted to know how to make soap, haven't you, Ren?"

I nodded my head up and down, pasting on a hopeful smile. Colette looked startled. She hadn't seen me since the night Mom had stormed the school. "Well, I—I don't know," she faltered. "I—" She glanced in dismay at her struggling cat and then at me again.

Clarissa's voice suddenly erupted from around the corner. "Good grief, Colette! Let those kids in and shut the door before Flim gets loose too." Colette gave a prim nod and motioned us inside. As soon as we crossed the threshold, Flam shot out of Hugh's grasp and dashed toward a tall round contraption that stood next to the cat's climbing structure near the piano.

"Cool!" Hugh exclaimed when Flam sprang up on the wheel and started running. "Is that a hamster wheel for cats?"

As if the scene wasn't already odd enough, Clarissa appeared at our side, brandishing a metal spoon and wearing safety goggles and rubber gloves. "We prefer to call it an exercise wheel," she corrected loudly with a thrust of her spoon in the air. "Bengal cats love to keep busy."

I watched, transfixed, as Flim bounded over to join his brother. They sprinted inside the ring together for a while, so fast that the spokes blurred. Then, like performers in a feline circus act, they took turns leaping off and back on again, somehow managing to keep the wheel smoothly spinning the whole time.

"Aren't they something?" Colette murmured proudly.

"Come on, Col," Clarissa interrupted before I could

answer. She bustled over to a stove and a metal-topped table tucked in the far corner of the room. "We don't want this batch to turn crumbly on us."

After Colette had scurried off, I flicked my hand at Hugh, shooing him toward the cats. He needed to pretend to keep watching them. Then once the sisters were distracted, he could drift away and snoop around. I quickly scanned the room, searching for things that might not have changed since Mr. Bonnycastle's day. There were some window seats lining the sunny alcove where the piano stood, but they didn't look like the kind with storage space underneath. I edged in the opposite direction of the stove, trying to get a glimpse past the cat wheel and the bamboo screens that divided the other end of the room.

Then I noticed Hugh in the alcove hopping up and down like he had to go to the bathroom.

"What?" I mouthed.

He pointed to the old upright piano and mimed lifting the lid on top and peering down inside. It was a good idea—except for one thing. I remembered Hildy mentioning she had let the sisters hire someone to come and tune the piano after they had moved in. If a box of pearls had been hidden inside the piano, the tuner would have been the first one to find it.

I shook my head at Hugh and motioned toward the bamboo screens. He scowled back at me, but there wasn't time for more hand signals. Clarissa was waiting. "Well, young lady," she shouted. "Do you want to learn how to do this or not?"

The sisters were making lavender-sage soap, and they were already deep into the process by the time I joined them at the stove. They hunched over their pots like witches, taking turns with explaining the basics—about lye powder and the sort of lard and oils and herbs they liked to use. I kept sneaking looks over my shoulder as Clarissa added a little honey for "better lather" and Colette demonstrated how much you had to stir to get the proper consistency. The cats must have had their fill of exercising. Now they were sprawled on the platforms of their climbing structure. Meanwhile Hugh had disappeared. A few minutes later I caught sight of him sliding around the corner of the screens. He gave me a helpless shrug.

"Ren!" Clarissa hollered. I jumped to attention. She was transferring her pots from the stove to the table. "Make yourself useful. Bring me those molds off the shelf over there." I collected the soap molds and then held them steady, breathing in the sweet-sharp vapors as the sisters ladled their purplish concoction into the long narrow pans. Once they had given each mold a good rap to get rid of air bubbles, they let me sprinkle lavender buds and ground sage leaves on top.

Colette clasped her hands together, admiring my work. "Perfect," she cooed. "Now we'll let those set for a day or so. Once the soap comes out of the molds, we cut it, wrap it in pretty paper and ribbon, and voilà . . . C & C Beauty Bars."

"C and C for Colette and Clarissa?" I asked, trying to keep my smile from turning into a laugh. With their plain-Jane faces and dowdy clothes, the sisters seemed like the least likely pair to spend their days making beauty products.

Clarissa was wiping her hands on her apron. "Now where'd that rascal Hugh get off to?" she asked.

"Uh—I'm not sure," I said. I took a few steps toward the alcove and peered around the corner. My heart leaped to my throat. Somehow Hugh had managed to lift the lid of the piano by himself, and now he was standing on the bench with his body stretched dangerously over the keys. He was so absorbed in searching the innards of the piano he didn't even hear me gasp.

Clarissa's bellow, however—as loud as a foghorn— couldn't be ignored. "What on earth!" she shouted when she saw what was happening, and Hugh jolted upright in surprise. I lurched toward him, but it was too late. The bench tipped and a jangle of sharp chords rang out as Hugh tumbled against the piano keys, sending Flim and Flam flying from their perches.

"Heavens, Hugh!" Colette cried, rushing forward. "Are you all right?"

He had landed on the floor with his spindly legs up in

the air. "I think so," he said shakily, after we had helped
him to his feet and he had inspected a spot on his elbow
and rubbed his knee. Clarissa seemed more concerned for
the piano than Hugh. Grimly closing the lid, she plinked
and plunked her way up and down the keys.

I bit my lip, listening for sour notes. "Is it okay?"

"Probably not," Clarissa grumbled. She tested middle C
a few more times. "What on earth were you up to, Hugh?"

When Hugh flicked his gaze toward me, I stared back
with my mouth frozen halfway open. "I—I don't know,"
he said. "I guess, well . . . I was trying to see how pianos
work. I've always wanted to play one."

Clarissa's eyes softened. "Well, why didn't you just say
so?" For once, her voice sounded as gentle as her sister's.
Before long, Hugh was sitting on the bench next to Clarissa, playing scales—and the cats were at it again, running on their wheel.

"Would you like to help me get the next batch of soap
started?" Colette asked me. She rubbed her hands together. "It's my favorite. Lemon rosemary oatmeal."

"Sure," I answered with a dreary smile. The Fortune
Hunters? Yeah, right. So far, Hugh and I were doing a
lousy job of living up to our name.

TWENTY

AT SAG ON MONDAY we all had to give the class an update on how our service projects were coming. Ollie told about the two hours she had spent walking dogs at the animal shelter on Saturday. Raymond said he had played basketball with kids at the neighborhood center. Arnold seemed especially pleased with his project. He was designing something called the "Time's-Up Zapper"—a remote-controlled device that would rid the world of people who hogged seats in public spaces like libraries. "One good jolt and they're out of there," he proudly explained.

"Hold on, Arnold," Stretch said. "You're supposed to be volunteering at the library. I don't think giving electric shocks to library patrons exactly qualifies as a community service."

"But shelving books is so boring," Arnold whined. Stretch ignored him and moved on, and of course Arnold decided to take his frustrations out on me a few minutes later. "Wait," he scoffed once I had finished describing my first day of work in the museum. "You actually think people are going to pay money to go in some old gym and look at a bunch of buttons?"

"Sure," I said, even though I could feel my face growing hot. "The way they made buttons a long time ago—it's really interesting. I've learned all sorts of cool stuff. Like I didn't know you could find pearls in shells from the river. The clammers used to find a bunch." I paused. "Well, not a bunch. They found slugs mostly. That's what they called the funny-shaped ones, but . . . anyway . . ." My voice dwindled as I glanced around the room. Everybody was staring at me like I was speaking a foreign language. If only I could tell them about Hildy's hidden treasure.

"Sounds fascinating, Ren," Stretch said before I could babble more. "Can't wait to buy my ticket." I sat down with a sigh, pretending not to notice Arnold's smirk.

Soon Stretch was clapping his hands together and unveiling the next assignment he had in store for us. We were supposed to design a diorama based on a favorite scene from a book we had read. *"Shadow boxes,"* he kept calling them, dipping his voice dramatically low—as if shadow boxes were something fresh and original instead of those same tired shoe boxes we'd been making since third grade with weird Play-Doh people falling over and Barbie furniture that didn't fit.

But after lunch, when Stretch wheeled in three carts full of art supplies, I was pleasantly surprised. The selection was a lot more creative than what I'd had to work with in elementary school. There were sturdy boxes in different sizes, real sculpture clay, roll-out sheets of fake grass and desert sand, and even bottles of something called Scenery Water. Everybody swarmed over, grabbing for what they needed.

Since I couldn't think of a scene I knew any better, I decided to do chapter 22 from *Little Women*. I scooped up drawing paper, colored pencils, and scissors from the supply cart, since I'd also decided to make paper-doll characters instead of molding them out of clunky clay. But as soon as I settled down to get started my hands turned heavy. Last night Mom had been in her bedroom for a whole hour talking on the phone. When she finally came out, her eyes were red-rimmed and swollen. "Who were you talking to?" I asked, steeling myself for the answer. "Aunt Ellen," was all Mom said, and I was afraid to ask more. Aunt Ellen was Mom's big sister who lived in Chicago—the one she called whenever she had a problem she couldn't solve on her own.

I set my pen down. I couldn't do it today—make myself draw Marmee and her daughters and their joyful smiles as the parlor door opens and they see Mr. March standing there, home from his long year away. I'd have to start with the wallpaper instead.

• • • • •

There was a spark of excitement in the air when I arrived at the school for my next Saturday of museum duty. Mayor Joy's rig was backed up to the front doors and he and Tucker and Garrett were carefully unloading something long and heavy wrapped in moving blankets. Hildy hovered in the foyer supervising. "Go slow now," she nagged. "Watch your step."

"What's going on?" I asked Hildy once the guys had headed toward the gym with their mysterious bundle.

"The Mayor hit the jackpot," Hildy told me. "A jewelry store was going out of business over in Smithton and he managed to convince the owner to donate his glass display cases to the museum. They're getting here in the nick of time. All week those fogies from the historical society have been calling, trying to make an appointment to see my collection. They wanted to come right away because they've got a board meeting on Monday and evidently I'm on the agenda."

It was a relief to hear the feistiness in Hildy's voice again and to see that she was back to her usual fashion habits. She had on hot-pink lipstick and a royal-blue tracksuit with silver trim. But from what I'd seen last week, the museum was nowhere near ready for its debut.

"So they're coming today?" I asked anxiously.

"No, thank heavens. I managed to hold them off till tomorrow. I wanted to stall as long as possible." She smiled mischievously. "Plus I knew asking them to come on a Sunday would be a good test. Those folks are so high and mighty. They wouldn't be driving out here on a day of rest unless they were serious about wanting to help."

I tried to catch Tucker's eye when he and Garrett and the Mayor returned for the next load, but he brushed by without even glancing in my direction. Apparently he was still miffed by the way I had fussed at him for being mean to Hugh. What a grump. It had been a whole week. He should have gotten over it by now.

"Where's Hugh?" I asked loudly, making sure Tucker could hear me out on the truck.

"Oh, he begged to stick around here and wait for you," Hildy said. "But there's a summer reading program at the public library in Bellefield this morning, and Mine said Hugh had to go so his brain doesn't turn to mush. They'll be back in a while."

Then Hildy and I headed to the gym so she could assign me my chores for the day. Halfway down the hall, I touched her arm and dropped my voice to a whisper. "Hildy, before I get started, do you think we could talk about the pearls for a second?"

She turned to face me. "Oh, Ren, honey. Are you still thinking you're going to track those down?"

"Of course," I said. "Hugh and I already started looking."

"Is that so?" Hildy jabbed her glasses higher on her nose. "When was that?"

"Last Sunday afternoon when you and Tucker were at the movies. We searched the whole basement."

"You *didn't*." Hildy let out a surprised chuckle and stared at me for an extra second. "It takes a lot of gumption to go down there. Did you see anything interesting?"

I grimaced. "Oh, it was interesting, all right. We searched every single room, but all we found was the sisters' cat. Then we decided to take Flam hostage so we could get inside the music room."

Hildy threw her head back and hooted.

"Things didn't really go like I had planned," I said. "The sisters had us so busy doing other stuff that we barely had a chance to look around."

"Oh, well." Hildy shook her head in amusement. "I don't think Tom would've hidden the pearls in the music room anyway, especially with so many kids coming in and out for classes. He would have picked somewhere more private."

"Like where? Were there any other places besides the basement where Bonny used to go? More out-of-the-way spots?"

"Well, he had an office up on the third floor—the room where Garrett lives now."

"Really?" I perked up.

"Yes, but that was one of the first places I looked, before Garrett ever moved in. I didn't find a thing."

"Anyplace else?"

Hildy pursed her bright pink lips, gazing at a spot over my shoulder and thinking hard. "He loved going up to the tower. I heard him chatting to Tom about it once. He said he could stay up there for hours watching the clouds go by."

"The tower!" I clapped my hands together. "I bet that's it. Did you ever try searching up there?"

Hildy winced. "I did. But to tell the truth, I barely made it off the stairs. I was afraid of giving myself a heart attack. Who knows if anyone would have ever found me." She lifted one thin eyebrow. "Now that I think about it though, the tower might be worth another look, but"—she pointed a crooked finger at me—"I don't want Hugh climbing up there. He's too unpredictable, and for all I know, that floor could be rotted through. You probably shouldn't be snooping around up there either for that matter."

Before I could argue, the guys came lumbering down the hall with another display case. "Bless you, Elton," Hildy said, patting the Mayor's arm as he shuffled past us. "I'm going to have more showing-off space than I know what to do with."

TWENTY-ONE

IN THE GYM Hildy pointed me to a plot of space she had staked out under the basketball hoop near the *Little Miss*. The wooden trunk I had seen on the balcony sat next to two card tables and folding chairs. Hildy motioned for me to take one seat while she took the other. Then she unlatched the lid of the chest and flipped it back. "*This* is what I need your help with today," she announced. "Sorting photographs."

It was hard not to make a face. The pictures, mainly black-and-white and grainy with age, were heaped in a hopeless jumble. Hildy said some were hers, but most had been passed down by Fortune's old-timers and ended up on her doorstep somehow, just like the specimens in her shell collection.

"How do I start?" I asked.

"For now, let's put them into categories," Hildy told me. "Then we'll pick out the best ones to feature in the display cases." She plucked up a photo from the muddle in the trunk and turned it over. "For example, here's one of a clamming camp down by the river. So this can be the clamming camp pile." She slapped the picture down on the corner of the card table next to me, then reached back in the trunk for another photo and began making more stacks and giving more instructions.

I forgot to listen for a second as I studied the clamming picture near my elbow. The camera had focused on a weathered-looking man in overalls who was bent over a workbench under the trees. A heap of shells and some tents filled the background behind him. "Is this your dad?" I asked when Hildy paused for breath.

"No, but my father spent a lot of his days in camps just like that one." Hildy pointed to something in the corner of the photo. "See that big metal tank? Once the clammers hauled in a load of mussels, they'd carry them up to a shady spot on the shore, dump them in a tank of water, and start a fire underneath. That's how they steamed the shells open so they could get the meat out."

"So is that how your father found all his pearls?"

Hildy nodded. "Pop was famous in Fortune for how fast he could work his way through a load of shells. His hands would fly, and he'd barely pause or bat an eye whenever he found a pearl. He'd just tuck it into his cheek like a wad of tobacco and keep going."

I wrinkled my nose. "He put the pearls in his *mouth*?"

"Yep." Hildy laughed. "It was the surest way to keep your pearls from getting snatched. There was a lot of thieving going on in those days." Her voice dipped low. "In fact that's how Pop's treasure started. With a little thieving of his own."

"Really?" I barely moved, afraid of doing anything that might break the spell of Hildy's storytelling.

Hildy set down the pictures she'd been holding. "Pop had worked in shelling ever since he was a little boy," she began. "At ten years old he was already earning his keep as a carrier, running buckets of shells back and forth. He found himself mixing with all sorts of unscrupulous types—the rowdy clammers and the pearl buyers who came through town. A lot of the buyers were swindlers, known for fixing their scales and measuring tools, and trying to trick the clammers into taking a lower price. There was one buyer in particular, a man named Peacock, who was notorious for cheating people."

Hildy stopped and listened for a minute, making sure the others were still occupied on the opposite side of the gym. "Whenever he conducted business," she went on, "Peacock would lay out a square of black satin so he could get a better look at the pearls—their quality and color. While most freshwater pearls were white, sometimes the buyers would come across different shades—everything from rosy pink to hints of green and blue. Well, one day when Peacock came through town, he couldn't resist showing off his latest prize—a large pearl with a rare salmon color that he'd bought from a clammer up in Wisconsin earlier in the week. The Blushing Beauty he called it, and he laid it out on his black cloth for his so-called friends in the tavern to admire. When they all crowded around to see, some young fellow who had had one too many bumped the table and the pearl went flying. There was a mad scramble, and when all was said and done the pearl was gone. Peacock raged and blustered and demanded everyone turn out their pockets. The search went on for hours, but my father was long gone with the Blushing Beauty in his hot little hand."

I drew in a sharp breath. "Your father took it? He was there?"

"Indeed he was." Hildy couldn't contain her crafty smile. "He had come to the tavern that afternoon to deliver a message to one of the clammers and he happened to be at the right place at the right time. He was so small and quick, only one or two people even noticed he was there. And since Peacock wasn't exactly popular in town, well, the police didn't worry themselves with a very thorough investigation."

"Wow. So your father kept the Blushing Beauty a secret all those years?"

"He had to," Hildy said, "if he didn't want to get caught. The story became pretty famous around here, and people would have recognized that pink pearl in an instant if he had tried to sell it."

"Did you ever see it? The Blushing Beauty? And the other pearls?"

"Not for years. I was a teenager in high school when Pop finally told me the story and showed me the wooden box that he kept them in. By that time, things weren't going so well for my father. My mother had died and the bottom was falling out of the shelling business."

Hildy paused long enough to give me a grave look. "That's about the time he started drinking." She turned and nodded sadly at the *Little Miss*. "He pulled his boat out of the water for good. Tom was the one who had to make ends meet. Even though business was winding down at McNally and Sons, Tom had managed to get a job in the office there. But cash was tight, and whenever Pop would run out of drinking money, he'd sneak off and sell a pearl or two."

"Not the Blushing Beauty."

"Oh, no. But he probably would have if Tom hadn't stepped in before he shipped off to join the army." Hildy shook her head ruefully. "Tom wanted to keep those pearls safe for me. But here I am still looking. My poor brother's probably rolling over in his grave."

"Hildy," I said, "I know you think it'd be a miracle if

we found that box. But what if we did? What would you do? Would you really sell the Blushing Beauty? It sounds so beautiful."

Hildy sighed. "You're right. If I ever find those pearls, it would break my heart to part with them again. But Tom meant them to be my nest egg"—she scanned the gym with a helpless laugh—"which would sure come in handy right about now." Then she slapped her hands on her knees and rocked herself to her feet. "But that's all silly talk. We got to keep thinking positive, and our best bet right now is making a good impression on those folks from the society."

Once Hildy had hurried off to see what the others were up to, I sat in a daze for a minute. After everything Hildy had told me, I was more determined than ever to sneak up to the tower and see if my instincts were right. But I knew I should bide my time until I could disappear without being noticed.

I reached in the trunk and pulled out a handful of pictures. So often I had wondered what Fortune was like in the old days, before it had turned to weeds and broken glass and crumbled stone. Now I could see. It was all there in the photographs—the clamming camps, the button factories inside and out, the bustling streets when business was booming.

I lingered over the details—the factory ladies' changing hair and dress styles and the way the swaggering young button-cutters posed with their caps cocked over one eye. When I came upon a manila envelope full of photos from former pearl button festivals, I pored over each one, searching the buildings in the background for features I might recognize. A little shiver went through me when I spotted a boy leaning out from a second-floor window of McNally and Sons, waving down at the parade passing by below.

Needless to say, I hadn't made much progress when Hugh came zipping around the corner an hour later and found me hovered over another batch of pictures. "Hey, what are you doing? Did you miss me?" he jabbered as he scooped up my stack of festival photographs. "Is this the pearl button festival? Is Hildy in any of these?"

"Not so far," I said, trying not to sound impatient as I reached out to take the pictures back. "But I've got a lot more to go through."

Hugh plunked himself down in the seat beside me. "Can I help?"

"I don't think so, Hugh. See, Hildy wants all the photos divided into categories." I gestured to the dozen or so stacks I had laid out across the two card tables. "And the system we've got going is kind of tricky. Sorry."

Hugh's face fell. He sat watching me in silence for a while, and then he whispered, "What about the pearls? I made Mine leave the library as fast as I could. Aren't we going to keep searching? You said you wanted to go back to Room 26 and look in those cabinets again."

"I know." I sighed loudly, pretending to be disappointed. "But I guess we're going to have to wait until after the visit from those historical society people. Did Hildy tell you about them coming tomorrow? I need to keep working so I can get these pictures organized in time."

Hugh crossed his arms and scuffed the toe of his sneaker against the floor.

"Why don't you go check with Garrett?" I suggested. I could hear the screech of metal on wood across the gym and Hildy's scratchy voice calling out orders. "Sounds like he might need some help over there."

"No way," Hugh muttered. "Tucker's already helping him."

Hugh drifted off, and a few minutes later I noticed him sitting inside the *Little Miss* with his chin in his hands. I tried to ignore the flicker of guilt rising in my chest. Hugh would love nothing better than hearing the tale of the Blushing Beauty and searching the tower with me. But now that Hildy had officially warned me, I couldn't risk taking him up there again.

When Mine came to the gym around noon and yelled that lunch was ready, I stood up slowly and stretched, peering over the boxes. Hugh was already plodding toward the door, and Tucker and Garrett were heading in the same direction. When I didn't join them, Hildy stopped by the card table to check on me.

"Time for a break," she said. "Aren't you coming? Madeline's gotten pretty good at making grilled cheeses."

I reached my hands toward the basketball hoop for another stretch. "No thanks," I said. "I ate a really big breakfast. I think I'll stay here and keep working."

"Well, be sure and come down to the kitchen if you get hungry," Hildy said as she turned to go.

"I will," I told her, even though I had no intention of changing my mind.

TWENTY-TWO

I HADN'T EXPECTED THE WIND. The corn had barely been stirring when I rode my bike to the school that morning. But now when I stole a look over the railing, the green stalks were bent almost sideways. I glanced up at the sky. No wonder Mr. Bonnycastle had climbed to the tower for cloud-watching. There were 360 degrees of them—puffy white wisps hung over Fortune, but off toward Bellefield the sky had turned the color of bruises.

At least the wind had driven the wasps away, and from what I could tell, the floor of the tower was completely sturdy. I dropped to my knees and crawled to the far left corner to get started. If Tom had hidden the pearls in the tower, I figured he would have pried up one of the boards and hidden the box in the hollow underneath.

The only way to find out, I decided, was to work my way from side to side, creeping back and forth until I had covered the four low walls under the railing's banister and all the floor space in between.

I couldn't help smiling at first. I knew I looked like a crazy person as I hunched over the boards, knocking here and there and hunting for raised edges and missing nails. But when a low round of thunder rumbled in the distance, I sat up in a panic to check my watch and the darkening sky. Luckily only ten minutes had passed since I'd left the gym and there wasn't any lightning yet. I crouched over the floorboards again.

By the time I finished searching the last corner, my knees were raw and I had two splinters lodged in the heel of my hand. "This is so stupid," I hissed, pushing myself to my feet in frustration. Mr. Baxter was probably right. The pearls were gone and most likely it was Mr. Bonnycastle who took them.

I must have stood up too fast because a sudden wave of dizziness rippled over me. I was tottering there, waiting for the floor to turn steady again, when something swooped down in the wind and brushed against my cheek. *A wasp.* I wheeled around, batting the air, and all at once I was stumbling forward and throwing my hands out to grab the rail. As I lurched against the banister I heard a sharp crack, and Hildy's warning about rotten wood came flooding back.

I froze for a long second, staring out at Garrett's half-finished labyrinth, the spinning pathway of shells and bloodred paint. Then, slowly, I moved my gaze downward. Between my hands, just at the spot where my stomach had landed, the railing was splintered and two of the spindles below it had slipped from their sockets and hung out over the slanted roof. I could feel the wood creaking under my rib cage. If I made a sudden move or leaned too far forward, the rail might give way. I squeezed my eyes shut and held my breath. Then, clenching every muscle, I shrank backward, inch by inch, until I was standing safely inside the tower again.

Who knows how long I sat on the dark steps under the trapdoor with my pulse pounding. I wasn't checking my watch anymore. *You could have died,* I kept thinking. If I had hit the railing just a little bit harder, I would have crashed through and . . .

I felt numb as I slowly groped my way to the bottom of the narrow stairs and stepped out on the third floor—almost like I was in a trance. It's the only way I can explain what happened next. When I noticed the door cracked open at the end of the hall, I didn't turn away and make a bee-line for the gym like a person in her right mind would have. Instead, I moved toward it, pushed the door open with one finger, and took a careful half step inside.

Garrett's room reminded me of a tidy ship's cabin, with each object tucked into a puzzle piece of space—a neatly made bed in one corner, a leather reading chair and ottoman in another, an antique desk lodged under the arched window in front of me. There were books and a teakettle and china teacups precisely arranged on the shelves in between. Right away I could see that if any pearls had been hidden in Bonny's old office, Garrett would have found them.

I took one more curious step toward Garrett's desk to get a better look at the patchwork of photographs that filled the walls on either side. They were labyrinths— bird's-eye views of all kinds—painted on stone floors or made with tile, etched into sandy beaches, outlined in the snow with Christmas lights, and carved into meadows and grassy lawns.

My trance snapped when someone spoke behind me. "What are you doing?"

I whipped around to find Tucker standing in Garrett's doorway with his arms crossed. My mouth wouldn't work at first. He waited coolly, his eyes pin-sharp and accusing through his bangs. "I—I don't know," I stammered. "Just being nosy, I guess. I needed a little break and I came up here to . . . to check out the tower and look around."

"You expect me to believe that?" Tucker's voice seeped with bitterness. "You're too much. First you lie to my grandmother and get her in all kinds of trouble with your mom. Then once you weasel your way back here with some lame excuse about a service project, you act all high and

196

mighty, telling *me*"—he tapped the tips of his fingers on his chest—"how *I* should act. But the whole time you're the one sneaking around, waiting till we go off to lunch so you can break into people's rooms."

"I didn't break in!" I cried. "The door was open. I've never stolen anything in my life. I swear! I was just looking at Garrett's pictures." I gestured limply back at the room behind me. Tucker rolled his eyes and turned away. "Tucker, wait!" I screeched as I hurried down the hall after him. "What are you going to do?"

"I'm going to tell Garrett that I caught you in his room. And I'm going to tell my grandmother that she's making a big mistake letting you come back here every weekend."

I had promised Hildy I wouldn't tell Tucker about the pearls, but I could feel the stored-up secrets bubbling inside me as I followed him down the steps. "You want to know why I've been sneaking around?" I shouted at the back of his head. "Because your own grandmother doesn't trust you!"

Tucker halted on the first-floor landing and slowly turned to look up at me. "What are you talking about?"

My knees felt weak. "It's a long story," I said.

"So I guess you better get started then." Tucker crossed his arms again. "Before somebody comes looking for us."

I sank down on the steps and told the story as quickly as I could, starting with the *no*s on the blackboards and

Hugh's spying and the letter in the safe and working my way toward how I ended up in Garrett's room. I tried not to get bogged down in details. I didn't even mention the Blushing Beauty.

At some point Tucker came to sit sideways on the step below me. He never interrupted once and he only asked a single question when I was finally done. "Why didn't Hildy tell me?"

"She was worried that you'd tell your dad."

"I'd never tell if she asked me not to," he said in a wounded voice. "I totally understand why Hildy doesn't want my dad involved. He has a certain way of looking at things. *His* way."

"But you hate it here, right? If you told your father about the pearls and all the money Hildy's spending, he'd probably make her sell this place and you could go home to your friends . . . and civilization."

Tucker pulled his chin back in disgust. "Is that really what you think I'd do? That I'd bail out on my grandma when she needs my help the most?"

"Sorry," I said quietly. "I guess I don't know you that well."

I looked up. Rain had started to spatter against the half-moon window high above the first-floor landing, and a flash of lightning illuminated the mural painted below—the children clamming by the river, the school off in the distance, the seagulls and puffy clouds. I leaned forward waiting for another flash to light up the inside sky. *The clouds.* I gasped and clambered to my feet.

"What is it?" Tucker asked. "What's wrong?"

"The mural," I whispered. I dodged around him, searching the shoreline in the bottom right corner of the painting.

"Lift me up," I said to Tucker as I rushed down to the landing.

"What?"

I hopped in place under the mural, staring up at the white scrawl of brushstrokes painted on the clump of grass in the corner. I pointed impatiently. "Come on. I need a boost so I can get close enough to see."

Tucker was shaking his head as he came down the steps to join me. But with a small sigh, he leaned forward and laced his fingers together over his knee. I was so focused on my mission I didn't even care that I was putting my nasty sneaker in Tucker's hands, bracing one palm on his shoulder and the other against the wall.

"Hurry," he groaned as I hefted myself up and tottered there for an unsteady instant, long enough to read the small signature that snaked across the clump of grass.

"That's him!" I cried.

"Who?" Tucker grunted as I jumped back down to the landing.

"Jonathan Bonnycastle! He's the one who painted that mural. I can't believe I didn't think of this before. Hildy told me he used to teach art lessons." I whirled around and stood on my tiptoes, scanning the tiny windows Bonny had painted across the front of the school.

"I don't get it," Tucker said. "What's the big deal?"

"Remember how I was telling you about the letter in the safe? About how Hildy's brother said the idea for the hiding place was right there under Bonny's nose? Well, maybe this is what Bonnycastle was doing that day— working on the mural—and maybe the clue is right here in the painting." I gnawed on my lip for a second, thinking about what to do next. "We've got to find a ladder. Come on!"

But halfway down the steps, I stopped and reached out to clutch the banister. "Hugh," I said. "Hi."

He was standing at the bottom of the stairs in the foyer. He swayed like a small ghost, staring up at me with his eyes shimmering. "You lied," he called out. His hollow voice echoed through the entrance hall. "You said you didn't have time to look for the pearls today. You said *we* were the Fortune Hunters."

Then, before I could stop him, he ran for the front door and shoved his way out into the storm.

TWENTY-THREE

I ASKED TUCKER to come with me. He knew the school property better than I did. Plus we could cover more territory with two people and we had to find Hugh fast. Lightning was still crackling across the sky, and each time I thought the storm had blown by, there would be another clap of thunder and more sheets of rain. We sprinted through the downpour, searching the obvious places first—the backseats of Hildy's van and Mine's station wagon, the cab of the Mayor's truck, the high grass in the old playground, and behind the lilac bush.

By the time Tucker and I met up again at the back of the school, the skies had settled to a drizzle. I stood on the edge of the cornfield, hoping to see Hugh's blond head pop up between the dripping rows. "Where could he have gone?" I groaned. I turned back to the labyrinth where

Tucker was standing on a leftover mound of shells, scanning the distance.

"We should check the Mayor's place," he said as he scrambled down the pile, sending shells clattering. I trotted after him. Straight back from the sisters' soap garden there was a narrow dirt lane through the corn that I'd never noticed before. We followed it and came out in a grassy clearing next to a stone building with a red tin roof and an open shed on one end. I didn't see any signs of the Mayor, but Wayne stood under the shed twitching his big ears and calmly munching from a pile of hay.

I was on my way toward the front door when Tucker touched my shoulder and twitched his chin at the shed. I looked over in time to catch a flicker of movement behind some hay bales that were stacked along the back wall. "I'll wait here," Tucker murmured, ducking under an overhang near the door. "He'll probably come out a lot faster if I stay out of the way."

I nodded and slowly headed into the shed, which was steamy with the smell of damp donkey hide. "How you doing, buddy?" I crooned in my best impression of the Mayor. I stood for a minute, rubbing the gray scruff between Wayne's ears and letting him nuzzle my pockets while I waited to see if Hugh would come out of hiding on his own.

He didn't.

"I know you're in here, Hugh," I called. "I'm sorry,

okay? Are you listening? I'm sorry I lied about what I was doing this afternoon. But it wasn't because I wanted to leave you out. I only did it because I wanted to go up to the tower to look for the pearls and Hildy told me it was too dangerous to take you along." I cocked my head, listening, but all I could hear was the rain pattering against the roof.

"Then I did something really dumb, Hugh," I went on. "Really dumb!" I paused. Maybe the suspense would lure him out . . . When that didn't work either, I marched across the shed and stood in front of the bales with my hands on my hips. "I went into Garrett's room without permission. Can you believe it? I didn't touch anything. I only looked around, but Tucker caught me. That's why I had to tell him what we've been up to, so he wouldn't squeal on me."

A sulky voice broke the silence behind me. "You never would have gotten caught if I'd been with you."

I swiveled around. Hugh was sitting high on the seat of an old farm tractor parked on the far side of the shed. "How'd you get over *there*?" I made my way toward him, weaving around a pile of scrap lumber and some stray hay bales. Hugh glowered down at me with his hands clenched around the tractor's steering wheel. He looked smaller than ever with his wet hair and clothes plastered against his skin.

"Hugh—" I flopped my arms at my sides. "That railing

in the tower was rotten. I almost fell through! And you're allergic to wasps, remember? Don't you see why I couldn't let you come?"

He glared over the steering wheel at the soaked pasture outside. "Where'd Tucker go? I saw him with you when you walked up."

Tucker slid around the corner of the shed with his hands in the pockets of his jeans. "Hey, Hugh."

Hugh didn't answer.

"Come on. Let's go back," Tucker said. "Don't you want to put some dry clothes on?"

Hugh pulled his knees up and hugged them, tucking his chin in between. "No way. You two can go find the pearls by yourselves." He sneered into his kneecaps. "Then you can go carve your names in the tower. Ren plus Tucker."

"Cut it out, Hugh," I said. He was acting ridiculous, but I couldn't keep from blushing anyway. Then out of the corner of my eye, I saw Tucker dig down in his jeans and pull out a pocketknife. He strolled over to the pile of lumber, picked up a piece of board, then sat down on one of the nearby hay bales and started whittling away.

I scratched at the back of my neck in embarrassment. "Um. What are you doing?"

"Carving," Tucker said. As Hugh watched in fascination, I edged closer to get a better view. I couldn't see the letters clearly at first, but then Tucker blew away the saw-dust and held up the board, leaning back to admire what he had carved so far: R + T +

Tucker thrust his knife in Hugh's direction. "Your turn," he said.

"My turn to what?" muttered Hugh.

"Why don't you come see?"

The pocketknife was too much for Hugh to resist. He slowly climbed down from the tractor and scuffed over to the hay bale where Tucker was sitting. Tucker handed him the board and Hugh blinked down at it. "You want me to add an H? For Hugh?"

"This is just practice," Tucker said as he passed Hugh the knife, handle first. "Whether we find the pearls or not, we should definitely go up to the tower and carve our initials this summer, right?"

My heart skipped with a little swell of surprise and relief. "Right," I agreed when Hugh didn't answer. "We should. As soon as Garrett fixes that railing."

Hugh was trying not to smile. He took the knife, hold-ing it stiffly in front of him like a tiny sword. He had just sat down on the hay bale next to Tucker when Wayne sud-denly let out one of his wheezy hee-haws. We all jumped, and the next thing we knew, the Mayor was striding into the shed, pushing back the hood of his rain poncho. "What're you kids doing out here?" he asked as he reached out to pat Wayne's flank. "Everybody's wondering where you got off to."

Hugh spoke up first. "We came to check on Wayne. I read somewhere that donkeys are really scared of thunder."

The Mayor's white eyebrows lifted. "Is that so? Well, Wayne looks like he survived, and you all need to be getting on back. Garrett's over at the gym waiting on you, Tucker. I'm afraid my back's done for the day and he needs more help with lifting." The Mayor took a few steps in Hugh's direction. "What are you up to over there?"

Hugh was already hunched over the board in his lap with his tongue poked out in concentration. "I'm carving," he mumbled. "Tucker loaned me his pocketknife."

The Mayor pulled off his poncho and waved his hand at Tucker and me. "You kids run along. I'll walk Hugh back when he's done."

The mud puddles in the lane lit up with a sudden flare of sunshine on our way back to the school. I glanced shyly at Tucker. "That was a good idea you had. The pocketknife."

"I knew it would work," Tucker said as he sidestepped a puddle. "Hildy gave me that knife when I turned eight. I thought it was the best present I'd ever gotten. My dad wasn't too happy about it though."

Hearing Tucker mention Mr. Baxter jolted me back to reality again. "So what do you think? Are we going to tell Hildy that you know about the pearls?"

"Yeah, I'll tell her tonight. But I don't think we should bring up your mural idea. It would only get her hopes up."

I stopped on the path next to the sisters' garden. "You think my idea's crazy, don't you? You think we're never going to find those pearls."

Tucker turned around with a smile playing along his lips. "Let's just say, I think it's a long shot."

I almost stomped my foot. He was as bad as his father. "Will you still help me though? I need to find a ladder. A really tall one."

"All right, all right." Tucker started down the path again. "I'll get you a ladder."

"Thank you," I started to say, but the words died on my lips as we rounded the corner of the school. My mother was standing on the front steps, reaching out to jab the buzzer. "Mom!" I called, running ahead. "What're you doing here?"

She spun around. "Oh, there you are! I left class as soon as I saw the lightning. I didn't want you riding your bike home in a thunderstorm." Then Mom noticed Tucker trailing behind me. "Who's this?" she said, folding her arms. Evidently she didn't recognize him from the night when she had barged in on dinner in the cafetorium. I could see her eyes darting back and forth, taking in our wet clothes, my bedraggled hair.

"This is Tucker, Mom. He's Hildy's grandson. He's here for the summer helping in the museum."

Mom didn't say hello. "So if you're both working in the museum, what were you doing outside? In a thunderstorm."

"The storm's over, Mom." I swiped my arm up at the sun breaking through the clouds. "See? I can ride my bike home. I'll be fine."

Before I could get any further, Hildy appeared. She barely greeted my mother as she wrestled the front door open and stepped out on the stoop. "Good grief. Where have you kids been?" she demanded. "You look like drowned rats."

Mom started marching down the steps. "Come on, Ren," she said. "Get your bike. It's time to go home."

"But, Mom, we've still got a lot of work to do—"

"I mean it. Let's go." She reached in her purse for her car keys. "I don't think Mrs. Baxter needs to be treated to another scene like last time, do you?"

No, I didn't. Without another word I retrieved my bike, and Mom helped me wedge it into the trunk of the car. I didn't glance up at the school again until I was slouched in the front seat with Mom's *First on Scene* textbook in my lap. Thankfully, Hildy had gone back inside by then, but Tucker was still standing on the steps. He lifted his hand in a sympathetic little wave as we pulled away.

We hadn't even bumped onto the paved road yet when Mom coughed out a dry laugh. "I really couldn't figure it out, you know. How determined you've been to keep going back to that place. It just didn't make sense, you spending every spare minute on the weekends helping some old woman make a museum—a *button* museum no less. But now I get it!" Mom took her hand off the steering wheel and thumped her forehead. "There's a boy involved. A really cute one."

Mom gave me a hard look as she turned left and picked up speed along the glistening river. "Seriously, Ren. I'm starting to get worried here. What exactly *were* you and that boy doing before I showed up?"

"*Nothing*, Mom," I said miserably. "Hugh ran away this afternoon so we had to go look for him. And you want to know what I did all morning? I sat in the gym for three hours going through old pictures. And then I skipped lunch so I could go crawl around on my hands and knees and get splinters and . . . and . . . oh, never mind. You don't know anything. Tucker's *not* the reason I've been going back to the school. I'd never go to all this trouble just to flirt with some boy I hardly know."

My words were still hanging in the air when Mom suddenly swerved off onto the shoulder of the road. I glanced around, startled. There weren't any other cars nearby. The only building in sight was an old silo covered with vines. "What's wrong? Why'd you stop?"

Mom didn't answer at first. She put the car in park and dropped her head back on the seat. Her face was welling with something strange as she blinked up at the upholstered ceiling. "I just realized," she breathed. "You know who you sound like, Ren?"

"Who?"

"*Me!* You sound exactly like me trying to defend myself about Rick. These last couple of months have been awful—the way you've been acting so suspicious and jumping to conclusions. But now here I am doing the same thing to you." Mom sat up straight and turned to me, her eyes pleading. "The thing is, Ren . . . we need to have faith in each other. We've got to stop assuming the worst when we have no idea what's going on." She reached forward and turned the car off, right there on the side of the road. "So tell me. Tell me about the school and I'll try to understand."

A few minutes later a nice man stopped to see if we had run out of gas or needed help, but my mother waved him away. I was just getting started and then, hopefully, it would be Mom's turn.

• • • • •

We stayed there, parked on the shoulder of the lonely road, for such a long time that we had to roll the windows down. Mom gave me the good news first: she had no plans to run away with Rick, or even date him, ever. "I'd be lying if I said I wasn't flattered by his attention at first," she told me. "But all along, I've been very clear with Rick that we're just friends." She squeezed my hands tight, so tight that it almost hurt. "Do you believe me?"

"Yes," I said, and squeezed back.

Then came the bad news. "You need to realize," Mom told me, "that your father and I might not get back together." Her words weren't a surprise. Still, hearing them spoken out loud, so clearly—with Dad's homecoming only two weeks away—felt like a kick in the ribs.

An army of peeper frogs had begun to trill in the ditch outside my window. "Why?" My voice melted into their cries. "You love him, don't you?"

"Yes," Mom said sadly. "But that's not enough sometimes."

"It's enough for Dad!" I reached my hand out the window and banged it on the outside of the car door. The ditch went silent.

"I'm so sorry, Ren. It's complicated. There're other issues that you're too young to understand right now."

Emotions twisted around inside me just like those vines swallowing up the silo down the road. Before the car ride, I had Rick to blame for our family coming apart. Now there was no one to blame but Mom.

"Can we go now?" I whispered.

"Sure." Mom nodded and reached out to squeeze my hand again, but this time I didn't squeeze back.

TWENTY-FOUR

AT LEAST I STILL HAD THE SCHOOL. Like a magic spell, my worries from home faded the minute I crossed the worn threshold the next afternoon. Hildy shook her head in astonishment when I walked into the gym. "Honey, you're like my birthday," she said. "Just when I think I've seen it for the very last time, it comes around again." But Hildy was too preoccupied to ask any questions about my mother's change of heart. Her visitors from the historical society were due in an hour.

I found myself beaming with approval as I glanced around the gym. The shelves of the display cases were lined with black velvet and Mine was carefully arranging items inside the last one in the row. Hugh had been assigned sweeping duty. And the Mayor, Garrett, and Tucker were dashing back and forth carrying garbage bags, cardboard boxes, clamming rakes, and burlap sacks full of button blanks.

"Wow, Hildy, everything looks great!" I gushed.

She sighed. "Well, it's about as good as it can get considering the amount of time we had. We stayed up half the night making things presentable. Even the sisters pitched in. They'd be here now, but they had to go peddle that soap of theirs at some craft fair."

"I would've stayed all night too if my mom had let me," I said longingly. "I'm really sorry I didn't get to finish sorting the pictures."

"Oh, don't worry. They're still over there waiting for you. Did you see any yesterday that looked like they belonged in a museum?"

"A lot. It was hard to pick, but I made a stack of the ones I thought were the best."

Hildy pointed to some empty picture frames that were piled on top of the display case where Mine was working. "There you go then. Have at it. Once you get the best ones in frames, we can set them out on those old clamming workbenches in the corner."

"What do you think?" Mine asked when I went over to collect the picture frames. I walked along the row of cases, peering at the array of shells and fancy buttons behind the glass. Hildy's button-queen picture and crown had a case all to themselves. The crown sat on a pink satin pillow. It was as tall as a chef's hat and it looked so heavy with decorations—buttons and pearls and rhinestones—I couldn't imagine how Hildy had managed to keep it balanced on her head.

"Gosh," I told Mine, "it almost looks like a real museum."

She laughed and glanced around to make sure Hildy wasn't listening. "I know, right? I have to admit I've had my doubts, but some of this stuff is actually kind of cool. Look." She held up a mother-of-pearl belt buckle. "Hard to believe a gnarly shell from the Mississippi River could turn into this." She knelt down and carefully laid the buckle on a shelf next to an iridescent tie clip and a pair of cuff links. I bent closer. There were fishing lures, a coin purse, a ladies' fan, and even a tiny revolver with its handle covered in chips of pearly shell.

Hugh came galloping over dragging his broom. "Did you see the gun?" he asked. "And what about *that*?" He pointed to an oversize pocketknife inlaid with mother-of-pearl and barely whispered, "Maybe we can borrow it when we go carve our names in the tower."

I flared my eyes at him in warning as I scooped up an armful of picture frames. Then I hurried off to my spot under the basketball hoop. But when I got there, the trunk and the card tables were nowhere in sight.

"Sorry," Tucker said as he came clanking up behind me. "We had to move all your stuff to the other side of the boat so we could make room for *this*." He banged one end of a long metal extension ladder down on the floor.

"You found one!" I said.

"Hildy's orders." Tucker smiled slyly and braced the top of the ladder against the backboard over our heads. "She wants Garrett and me to take down the hoops and the scoreboard because she says they don't go with her button theme." Then he paused. "I wasn't sure if you'd be needing this anymore or not. After yesterday, I didn't think we'd ever see you again."

"Yeah." I shifted the picture frames in my arms with an awkward laugh. "My mother kind of misunderstood what was going on."

"What do you mean? What did she think was going on?"

"Oh, who knows?" I said in a fluster, and rolled my eyes. "She completely overreacted." I lowered my voice, desperate to change the subject. "What about Hildy? Did you tell her? That you know about the pearls?"

"Yep."

"What'd she say? Was she mad at me for blabbing?"

"No. She actually apologized for keeping it a secret for so long. And she says it was silly for her to worry about my dad finding out since he already thinks she's bonkers anyway." Tucker shook his head with a gloomy laugh. "It was kind of sad. She told me that she's pretty much given up on ever finding the pearls. That's why I didn't mention your mural idea. My father would freak if he found out I was encouraging her."

I nodded solemnly. Hildy wasn't mad and Tucker trusted me a little more now. I didn't want to press my luck by asking him for anything else. "Thanks for showing me the ladder," I said as I turned to go. "Hugh and I can figure out the rest."

"Oh, I don't know." Tucker sounded doubtful as he lifted up one of the rungs. He started to grin. "This thing's pretty heavy. You two might need some help carrying it up those stairs in the hall."

I turned back with a little hop, rattling my picture frames. "Really?" I whispered. "You'll help us? When can we go?"

Later, Tucker mouthed as Garrett came around the corner, slapping a wrench against his palm.

Luckily we had the buzzer at the front entrance to give us a heads-up before the visitors stepped into the gym. While Hildy sent the Mayor out front to greet them, the rest of us scurried about making frantic finishing touches. I adjusted my assortment of pictures on top of the clamming bench. Tucker stashed the ladder in the storage room. Hugh hid his broom. Garrett gathered up the rusty bolts from the basketball hoops and Mine made a desperate attempt to finger-comb the mannequins' ratty blond hair. Then we all scattered to different corners, pretending not to watch as Hildy shook hands with her guests and launched into her first official button museum tour.

As soon as I laid eyes on the pair from the society, I was worried. The man had a long, prudish face, and he kept his hands clasped behind his back as he turned stiffly to study each piece that Hildy pointed out. And the woman reminded me of a Pekingese, with her snub nose and poufs of blond hair and the way she tip-tapped along in her tiny high heels. All she needed was a little pink bow on the top of her head. At least she seemed to be smiling some, but when she spoke she didn't sound so friendly anymore. She yapped out her questions in a high, tight voice.

"I'm not seeing any labels or captions here, Mrs. Baxter," I heard her say when they stopped by the display cases. "Do you have documentation for these pieces?"

"Oh, I know where everything came from," Hildy told her. "We just haven't gotten around to typing up the labels yet."

Once the visitors had circled around the gym, inspecting the button company signs and the sorting and polishing machines, Hildy brought them over to see the *Little Miss*. I shrank back in my chair, searching for an escape route. I'd been sitting quietly behind the card tables pretending to sort more pictures, but now that Ms. Pekingese was clicking toward me, there was nowhere to hide.

While her partner lingered by the boat, peering down

his nose at the hooks on the clamming rig, the woman seized a stack of photographs from the table and began thumbing through them. She flipped me a brief smile as she set the first stack down and snatched up another. "Fascinating," she said. She spun on her heel. "Mr. Vanderveer, you should take a look at these."

Hildy came over too and tried to introduce me, but the visitors weren't the least bit interested in why I was there. They huddled together like hens clucking over the photographs. Then, finally, Mr. Vanderveer straightened his narrow shoulders and fixed Hildy with a somber gaze. "Mrs. Baxter, you've amassed quite a collection here," he began. "These photographs are particularly extraordinary. But I must tell you, we're very concerned about preservation." I felt like I was watching a fun house mirror. His face stretched even longer. "Artifacts such as these require careful handling. Constant monitoring of climate and light exposure." He pulled a handkerchief from the pocket of his suit coat and dabbed at his forehead as he drearily turned to survey the gym.

"Absolutely," Ms. Pekingese yapped, staring pointedly at me. I slowly slid the photo I'd been holding back on the table.

"The fact is," Mr. Vanderveer went on, "we strongly believe artifacts of this magnitude should be housed in the town museum where they can be properly cataloged and preserved."

Hildy had her fists on her hips now. "So that's what the two of you have come here to tell me? That you want me to turn my entire collection over to that stuffy society of yours?"

Mr. Vanderveer drew himself up, exchanging an indignant look with Ms. Pekingese. "Of course you would be consulted every step of the way—"

"But if I turn my collection over to you," Hildy said, "nobody would ever see it. You people run that place of yours like Fort Knox. Don't folks have to make an appointment to get in?"

"Appointments are required, yes." Mr. Vanderveer nodded gravely. "But we open our doors to the public for a full week during Summerfest."

Hildy had grown very still. Her dark eyes glimmered behind her glasses as she stared up at him, considering. "One week," she repeated at last. "That's not enough for me, Mr. Vanderveer. Most of these treasures of mine are seeing the light of day for the first time in decades. The last thing I want to do is bury them all over again in that vault of yours in Bellefield."

I hadn't realized I was clenching the sides of my chair until Hildy was done talking. And now I could barely keep from giving her a standing ovation. The visitors, on the other hand, looked like they had each taken a gulp of sour milk.

"No matter," Hildy said briskly, as she began herding

them toward the door. "If you all can't help me, I'll find somebody else who can."

I resisted the urge to stick out my tongue when Ms. Pekingese took one last hungry glance back at the table full of pictures. As soon as Hildy had disappeared down the hall with the visitors, the rest of us gathered by the *Little Miss*.

The Mayor ran his palm over the top of his bald head. "Well, that sure didn't go like we had hoped, did it?"

"No, but I have to say Hildy was marvelous." Garrett chuckled. "She certainly put those prigs in their places."

Hugh began strutting along the side of the boat, doing a perfect impression of Mr. Vanderveer with his nose in the air and his hands clasped behind his back. Everybody laughed, but the mood in the gym turned solemn again once Hildy returned. She looked so exhausted that Tucker ran to get her a folding chair and Mine sent Hugh to the kitchen for a glass of water.

"Well, I suppose that's that." Hildy sighed as she lowered herself into the chair. "I probably burned my last bridge with those two."

"Are you sure?" Mine asked. "I thought you said the historical society had grant money to give away. Aren't there some forms I could help you fill out?"

Hildy snorted. "Did you see the looks on their faces when they walked out of this place?" She shook her head. "Filling out a bunch of forms isn't going to help. They want me to donate my collection to *them*. Not the other way around."

Hugh arrived with the glass of water, and we all hovered around Hildy's chair trying to cheer her up until she finally swatted the air with her hand and told us to go about our business. "No need fussing over me anymore," she said. "I'll get my second wind in a minute."

My breath caught with excitement when Tucker wiggled his eyebrows at me and darted a glance toward Hugh and then the storage room. Now more than ever we needed to track down those pearls for Hildy. I slipped my hand in my pocket and gave my button blank a squeeze. I was glad I had remembered it when I got dressed that morning. With any luck, the key to Hildy's mystery was only a short climb away.

TWENTY-FIVE

THERE WAS NO QUESTION about who would go up on the ladder. Inspecting the mural was my idea in the first place, right? And ever since I had spotted Mr. Bonnycastle's signature, I'd been itching to climb up and scour the painting for clues. From the landing, the school in the background appeared hazy, as if it was shimmering in the heat, but I was sure some hint would reveal itself once his brushstrokes—in the words of Hildy's brother—were right under my nose.

Tucker hardly had time to set the ladder into place before I gripped the metal sides and started climbing. But by the sixth rung, my palms were sweaty and the stairwell felt like it was heaving up and down underneath me.

"What's wrong?" Hugh asked. "Why'd you stop?"

"I don't know," I moaned. "It's so stupid, but I'm already dizzy. I think that tower must have given me a phobia." Somehow I had turned into a complete wimp overnight. I tried lifting my foot to take another step.

"Whoa," Hugh said. "I can see your legs shaking."

"You want to come down?" Tucker asked. "I can do it."

"Okay," I said with a resigned sigh, and slowly picked my way back to solid ground. "But you've got to be serious about this. We don't want to miss any clues."

"Whatever you say, Sherlock," he teased as he took my place on the ladder.

At least at the start of his inspection, Tucker seemed like he was trying to do a thorough job. He combed his gaze along each little window Bonnycastle had painted on the school and he leaned in close to inspect the tower on top. But after he had shifted the position of the ladder two or three more times, he jumped down to the landing with a shrug. "Sorry, Ren. There's nothing up there." Even Hugh had lost interest. He sat on the steps writing his name in the dust in the corner of the stairwell.

"But we're not done yet! What about that side?" I pointed to the left half of the mural where the children were painted. Something on the small stretch of sand in the foreground had caught my eye—some sort of rectangular box.

Tucker's shoulders slumped. "Seriously? Come on, Ren. I told Hildy we'd be back in a few minutes."

"Please, Tucker," I begged with my palms pressed together. "Just one more minute. That box on the shore looks like it has writing on it."

"What box?" Tucker glared up at the mural. "*That?* That's a picnic basket."

"No, it's not," I snapped. "It's too big and there's no handle."

Hugh hopped to his feet to see what we were talking about. "Maybe it's a treasure chest," he said. "Want me to look, Tucker? I love heights."

"No, I'll do it," Tucker growled. He dragged the ladder across the landing and had barely trudged up the rungs again before he announced flatly, "Like I said, it's a picnic basket."

"Those aren't letters on the front?" I asked stubbornly.

"No, it's supposed to look like wicker or something. I don't know," Tucker said impatiently. "Whatever those marks are, they're definitely not letters."

Hugh gave the wall under the mural a glum little kick. "So much for that idea," I muttered. I waited for Tucker to leap off the ladder and say "I told you so," but for some reason he had frozen in place. "Aren't you coming down?" I asked. "What are you looking at?"

Tucker tapped his finger on one of the boats in the mural—the one closest to the children on the shore. "This boat. It's got a name painted on its side."

"Really?" I waited. "Well, what is it?"

"I don't know. The writing's really tiny." Tucker leaned closer, squinting. "Uhhh . . . it's got five letters and it says . . . it says . . ." Then he stood up straight on the ladder. "It says *Pearl*."

Hugh began to pace in a circle around me as I gaped up at Tucker with my thoughts reeling. "So all this time the pearls weren't in the basement or the tower or Room 26 or anywhere else in the school!" Hugh said, throwing his arms in the air. "All this time they've been on some boat named *Pearl*!"

I grabbed Hugh's elbow to make him be still. "Or maybe . . . maybe they're here after all. Maybe Tom hid them on his father's boat! The one that's sitting right down the hall in the gym."

Tucker came down to the landing, looking baffled. "What? What do you mean? That boat in the gym belonged to my great-grandfather?"

I gawked at Tucker in surprise. "Yes. Didn't Hildy ever tell you that? It was Pop's. And if you think about it, everything makes sense! Hildy said her dad retired from clamming when she was in high school. And she talked about how sad it was when he pulled his boat out of the water for good. And all that happened before Tom went off to war."

"Hey . . . now I remember." Tucker's voice filled with wonder. "There used to be an old boat in the barn behind Hildy's house. I always wanted to play on it when I was

225

little, but it was mostly covered up with junk back then—all of Hildy's button stuff. I never asked any questions about it because I wasn't ever supposed to go inside the barn. Dad thought I'd fall on something and get hurt."

"But, you guys," Hugh sputtered, "it's not the same boat. The boat in the gym is called *Little Miss.* Not *Pearl.* And it's green and white. That boat up there is—is—" He stepped up on the bottom rung of the ladder to double-check. "Gray!"

We were still debating, talking so loud that the Mayor almost had to shout Tucker's name before any of us noticed him standing at the bottom of the stairs.

The Mayor's face softened when we all fell silent. "I'm sorry, son," he said gently. He gripped the newel post, trying to catch his breath. "You need to come to the gym. Your grandmother's had a bad fall."

TWENTY-SIX

HUGH STUCK BY MY SIDE once Tucker ran pounding down the hall. He was staying quiet like a small, stunned animal. "What should Hugh and I do?" I asked the Mayor.

"You two wait out front for the ambulance," he told me. "Once the paramedics get here, you can show them how to get up to the balcony."

"The balcony?" My voice came out quivery and I pressed my knuckles to my mouth. "What happened?"

"Hildy says she was up there trying to find her type-writer." The Mayor shook his head in sad disapproval. "I guess she tripped or lost her footing somehow. It's a blessing that I came back to the storage room for another load of trash. That's when I heard her yelling for help."

I barely felt my legs carrying me outside to the after-noon sunshine. It was all my fault. Hildy probably wanted that typewriter to make labels for the display cases. If we had stayed in the gym, one of us could have run to the balcony and found it for her.

"Hildy must be hurt bad," Hugh said when we finally heard the siren screaming along Old Camp Road. He nudged closer. It was scary—those red lights flashing and the siren's wail cutting across the hush of the cornfield. The ambulance jerked to a stop at the end of the walkway and Rick bounded out of the front seat. *Of course.* My nerves were so jangled I'd completely forgotten that he might be on rescue squad duty that day.

"Ren," he said as he hurried toward me. "Are you all right?"

I nodded. As much as I thought I despised him, my throat welled with relief at the sound of his calm, familiar voice. Behind him, the back doors of the ambulance sprang open and two more members of the rescue team emerged, sliding out the stretcher.

Garrett came running around the side of the school with the weed whacker banging against his legs. "What happened?" he asked as he hurried toward us in confusion.

"It's Hildy." My voice had turned froggy. "She fell in the gym."

Hugh trotted a little ahead of me as we showed Rick and the other paramedics where to go. But once we reached the steps that led to the gym balcony, I grabbed Hugh's hand and pulled him aside, motioning the way. I didn't want Hugh to see Hildy in pain, lying on the dusty floor. And I couldn't stand to see her either. Imagining the scene was bad enough. I was grateful when Mine came hurrying down the stairs to usher Hugh and me back to the library.

"I think she might have broken her hip," Mine told us. "That happens a lot with old people. But don't worry." She hugged Hugh to her side and reached out to squeeze my shoulder. "Hildy's a trooper. She'll be fine." Then Mine asked if I would stay with Hugh while she drove Tucker to the hospital to be with his grandmother. "I won't be gone more than an hour or so," she added. "I'll ask Mayor Joy or Garrett to tag team with me."

Once Mine left, we stayed in the library until the shriek of the sirens had faded away. Then we went back to the landing to get the ladder. The color of the mural had darkened in the long gold shadows of the afternoon. I caught myself staring up at the boat named *Pearl* as we took the ladder down. Hugh followed my gaze.

"Should we go look?" he whispered. "Inside the *Little Miss*?"

"I don't know," I wavered. I pictured Tucker sitting in a hard plastic chair in the emergency waiting room. "Don't you think we should wait for Tucker?"

"I bet he'd want us to go ahead and look," Hugh reassured me. "Think how happy Hildy will be if we find the pearls. We could bring them to her at the hospital and she'd get better a lot faster."

I couldn't argue with that. Together, we hoisted up the ladder and soon we were back in the gym, throwing our legs over the side of the *Little Miss.* Hugh started in the bow while I took the stern. "Check all the floorboards," I told him. "And make sure to knock and listen for hollow sounds."

Hugh squatted down. "Because there might be a secret compartment, right?"

"Right. But don't get your hopes up," I warned. Out in the stairwell, the boat had seemed like a great idea for a hiding place. But now I wasn't so sure. With its flat bottom and splintery sides, the *Little Miss* was about as plain as you could get. I couldn't see a single nook or cranny where the box of pearls might be hiding. Still, Hugh and I got to work, crawling along on our knees and rapping our knuckles against the deck and the sides. It sounded like a flock of woodpeckers had invaded the gym. I paused to examine a few suspicious chinks in the wood, but my spirits were sinking by the time I bumped up against Hugh in the middle of the boat.

I pushed myself to my feet and trudged over to sit on the bench that stretched across the stern. When something squeaked, I froze for a second, and then bounced up and down a few more times. It wasn't a wood squeak. It was a rusty-hinge squeak. I leaped up and tugged at the top of the bench, and sure enough, the lid screeched open. Hugh thudded along the deck to join me and we both knelt down in front of the storage space, peering inside.

"Shik," Hugh said. "It's empty."

We spent another minute squinting into the dim corners and reaching over to thump on the water-stained floorboards. But like the basement and the music room and the tower, the bench didn't hold a single glimmer of pearls or any hope of ever finding them. I closed the lid, feeling guiltier than ever. The mural had been a wild goose chase. And now Hildy was in the hospital.

"I don't know, Hugh," I said as I climbed out of the boat and dismally dropped to the floor. "I hate to be a quitter, but maybe we just need to face facts. Hildy's treasure is gone."

Hugh was right behind me. "No, it's not gone," he insisted. "It's hidden on a boat called *Pearl*. We just need to look all over Fortune until we find one!"

"We'll see," I said. I couldn't even pretend to smile.

"So what do you want to do now?" Hugh asked once we had propped the ladder against the wall in the storage room. "You want to go see how the labyrinth's doing?"

"I don't think so." I sighed. The memory of the labyrinth yawning up at me as I hung over the railing in the tower flashed through my head. All those spirals winding round and round . . . My brain was in enough of a muddle already. Visiting the labyrinth would only make things worse.

"We could go eat something," Hugh said.

I shrugged. "Sure. Why not?" But just as I expected, the cabinets in the kitchen didn't offer too many choices. Hugh's face scrunched when I showed him the options— dried apricots, raw almonds, or canned lentil soup. "How about some scrambled eggs?" I asked after I had inspected the shelves of the refrigerator. "I'm pretty good at those."

Hugh shook his head. Then his gaze wandered to the top of the fridge. "What about Lucky Charms?" he whispered.

"It's not your birthday," I reminded him. "It's not even your half birthday."

"Don't worry. Mine'll understand." He was already sliding a chair over so he could reach. We each ate two bowls full. Hugh had clinked his spoon down with a satisfied sigh and was lost in studying the back of the cereal box when we heard a jingle of keys and a man's voice echo through the cafetorium. "Hello? Anyone home?"

I stood up from the table and peeked through the serving window. My stomach lurched with dread. *It couldn't be.* Less than two hours had passed since Hildy's accident. Her son couldn't possibly have made it all the way from Des Moines that fast. But there he was. Mr. Baxter— walking toward me with his head bent to the side as if he couldn't quite believe his eyes. "Wait," he said. "Aren't you that girl who—"

"I'm Ren," I said before he could finish his sentence. "Ren Winningham."

He blinked at me. "I don't mean to be rude, but what are you doing here? The last time we met your mother made it very clear that she didn't want you anywhere near this place."

"Oh, that was all a big mix-up," I told him. "My mom lets me come help in the museum every weekend now." I nodded toward the end of the table where Hugh was trying to disappear behind the Lucky Charms box. "And Mine asked me to stay with Hugh until she gets back from the"—I hesitated. What if he didn't know yet? What if he had made the trip for some other reason?—"until she gets back," I said weakly.

Mr. Baxter leaned through the window. "Hello, Hugh," he said brusquely. Hugh finally poked his head out and gave a little wave. "Tucker told me your mother drove him to the hospital. That was kind of her."

My chest fluttered with relief. At least I wouldn't have to be the one to deliver the bad news. Mr. Baxter reached up and loosened his tie. "I stopped by to get some of Mother's things before I head over there. It sounds like she'll be staying a few nights."

A few nights? I wanted to ask more about Hildy, but I kept silent. Questions would only keep him there longer, and for some reason, he was turning to look at me again with that same suspicious glint in his eye. "Were you here?" he asked. "When my mother fell?"

I nodded.

"Did you see how it happened?"

"No," I answered softly. "We were . . . somewhere else."

"We? Who's we?"

"Um." I could feel beads of sweat gathering on my upper lip. "Hugh and me . . . and Tucker." As soon as I said Tucker's name, Mr. Baxter's face darkened. He pressed his palms flat on the counter outside the window like a police detective searching for patience. "You say you were somewhere else? Where were you?"

I swallowed. "We were out in the foyer. On the stairs."

"And what, may I ask, were you doing out there?"

I stole a glance at Hugh, who looked like he'd been caught in a game of freeze tag.

"What were you doing on the stairs?" Mr. Baxter demanded again.

"We were just . . . hanging out, I guess. Just messing around."

"Hanging out? Messing around?" Mr. Baxter exaggerated each syllable. "Do you know, Miss Winningham, why my son is here this summer?"

"To help Hildy in the museum?" I said in a thin voice.

"That's right," Mr. Baxter snapped. "He's not here to socialize, especially when his grandmother is rattling around by herself in that godforsaken gym."

"I know," I said in a rush. "We weren't gone that long. We only went out to the stairway for a few minutes."

"Well, that's not much comfort at this point," Mr. Baxter interrupted. "My mother may have broken her hip. Who knows if she'll be able to bounce back from this?"

I was struggling with how to answer when Mine swept into the kitchen in a blur of dreadlocks and scarves and hospital smells. Hugh ran over to hug her, almost knocking her off balance. "Hey, mister," she said as she steadied herself and stooped to hug him back. "What's going on?" She scanned the room in bewilderment. "Wow! Mr. Baxter. You're here already. How'd you make it so fast?"

Mr. Baxter scratched impatiently under his collar. "I was meeting with a client who lives about an hour west of here. I usually don't work on Sundays, but now I'm glad I did."

Mine nodded. "Mayor Joy and Garrett are still at the hospital. They're keeping Hildy and Tucker company while they finish all the tests and stuff. So I came back to check on how the kids were doing." Her gaze skimmed over the Lucky Charms box, then rested on me. I knew she could see it—me, fighting not to cry.

"Your timing's perfect," Mr. Baxter was saying. He glanced irritably back at the stage. "I have no idea where Mother keeps anything around here. Her toothbrush. Medications. Maybe you can give me a little direction."

"Sure," said Mine. She cupped Hugh's chin in her hand

and tipped his head back. "Don't go anywhere. I'll only be a few minutes."

Once they had gone, Hugh folded his arms, scowling. "Tucker's got a mean dad."

"He *was* mean," I said with my voice wobbling. "But he's probably only acting that way because he's worried about Hildy."

"No, I could tell he was mean already. He's got pointy ears."

I covered my face with my hands for a second, not knowing whether I was going to laugh or sob. "Listen, Hugh," I said. I sucked in a big breath of air. "I've got to go. Mom's probably wondering why I'm not home yet."

"Mine could give you a ride," Hugh offered.

"No, that's okay." I began edging toward the door. "I'd rather ride my bike. Will you tell Mine for me?" He nodded. "Bye, Hugh," I called over my shoulder as I hurried down the hall. I knew he'd probably follow me all the way to the front steps, so I didn't let myself look back once as I rushed outside and climbed on my bike. And I didn't slow down until I was at the end of the school driveway.

There was one thing I had to do before I pedaled away. Climbing off my bike, I reached in my pocket. Then I reared back and threw, harder than I've ever thrown before. High in the air, my button blank caught the sunlight before it disappeared into the rows of corn.

TWENTY-SEVEN

WHENEVER THE PHONE RANG on Monday evening, I was sure it was Mine or Garrett or maybe even Tucker calling to tell me Hildy was okay. My heart dropped each time it turned out to be a salesman on the line or one of Mom's friends. My only news about Hildy came from Rick, who had a friend who worked at the hospital. The details were spotty. All I knew was that Hildy "was recuperating," but Rick's friend had no idea when she'd be coming home.

Mom offered to take me to the hospital to visit, but I was too worried I might run into Mr. Baxter there. So we sent flowers to her room instead, and Mom asked the florist to sign my name on the card. By Tuesday night, I was convinced. Mr. Baxter must have made it clear that I was banished from the school. And Tucker had probably gotten in so much trouble for "hanging out" instead of helping Hildy that he never wanted to see me again.

Strangely enough, I began to look forward to going to SAG that week. Anything was better than staying at home stewing and pedaling my bike aimlessly around the neighborhood, wondering if I'd ever be riding out to the school again. After thinking shadow boxes would be the biggest waste of time ever, now I couldn't wait for each afternoon when I got to work on my diorama and escape to the cozy world of the Marches' parlor.

The fireplace was taking forever, but I didn't care. On Stretch's supply cart there was special foam in different shades of red—perfect for brick-making—and for two peaceful hours on Wednesday afternoon, I didn't think about Hildy lying in her hospital bed or the museum gathering dust or Mr. Baxter's face twisting with anger. All I thought about was creating my tiny bricks, molding and pinching and then cementing each one into place on the hearth with superglue.

On Thursday I was working on the mantel, trying to make my raw stick of wood look like mahogany, when Stretch decided it was time for a talk. He grabbed a chair across the table, spun it around, and sat down with his arms laced over the back of the seat. "So, Ren," he began. "Your stomach's feeling better, I take it."

"A little bit better," I said wanly. Earlier that day, when Stretch said it was time for our weekly service project updates, I had pretended to have a stomachache and hid in the bathroom until everyone went to lunch.

"Are you feeling up to giving us a report this afternoon?" Stretch asked.

"Do you think I could maybe do it tomorrow?"

"We're not here tomorrow, Ren." Stretch's usual perkiness was dampening. "It's a holiday, remember? The Fourth of July?"

"Oh. Right."

He gave me a skeptical look. "Okay, let's have it. What's going on?"

I stared down at the little pools of paint I had squeezed on my plastic tray—brown and black and white. If only the rest of my life could be so simple and straightforward. "I don't think I can go back to the museum," I said.

Stretch's eyes widened in surprise. "Why not?"

I couldn't tell him the whole story. It had been hard enough trying to explain everything to Mom. So I gave him the short version. "There's probably not even going to be a museum," I said. "The woman who owns it, Hildy, she fell last weekend and I think she might still be in the hospital."

Stretch winced sympathetically. "That's terrible. You don't know when she'll be going home?"

I shook my head.

"Well, I bet your friend Hildy is going to need more help than ever once she gets out of the hospital. The museum might not work out, but you could lend her a hand with other things, right? Sure sounds like community service to me."

"I guess so," I murmured.

Stretch gave me a thumbs-up sign. "So let's shoot for a report on Monday, okay?"

I nodded and picked up my paintbrush. I'd have to think about Monday later. For now, all I needed to worry about was finishing my mantel with its tiny Christmas stockings and creating the tissue-paper fire underneath. That way I'd have all next week to figure out the people— the sisters and Marmee and Father—before SAG ended and before Dad came home.

• • • • •

Dad loved the Fourth of July. He kept the same ritual every year. Each June, he and Uncle Spence would drive all the way across the border to Missouri, where it was legal to buy fireworks. They kept it secret what they bought, always claiming that this year's show would be the best ever. The suspense would build throughout the day. First we'd have a cookout for friends in our back-yard. Then we'd troop to City Park to watch the Jaycees put on their annual fireworks extravaganza. And at last, while everyone else headed home, tired and satisfied, the

Winningham family would drive out to the country to see our own private fireworks display.

It happened in a field overlooking the river on the other side of Fortune, where my father had permission to hunt and wander with Old Blue whenever he wanted. Mom, Nora, and I would sit on the hood of the car clapping and cheering while off in the distance my father and his brother sprinted around in the dark like teenagers, lighting off their stash.

Of course I knew the Fourth wouldn't be the same this year. I didn't feel like going to the park without Dad. Uncle Spence had other plans, and there'd be no fireworks in the field. "Since we're not doing anything," Nora said as she sat at the counter eating toast that morning, "can I go hang out with Alain? His host family's having a party so he can see all of that rah-rah USA stuff before he goes back to France. You know, like hot dogs and a flag cake and sparklers . . ."

Mom and I had been emptying the dishwasher. She swung around with a glass in her hand. "But we *are* doing something," she said. "There's a big get-together for all the military families at the rec center this afternoon. They're having a barbecue and everyone's going to make welcome-home banners."

I stopped plunking forks into the silverware drawer. "You actually want to go to that?" I asked.

"Of course I do, Ren," Mom said with a sigh. She dropped her arm, letting the glass dangle at her side. "I can't wait for your father to get back home, safe and sound. Don't you know that? No matter what happens between Dad and me, we're still a family, right?" She gave Nora a firm look. "So we're going to go make banners. You'll have to wait and see Alain tomorrow."

Nora didn't argue. "Okay." She sniffed and went back to eating her toast. I wanted to be that way—to be able to give a little shrug and get on with life. But in my head, the reunion movie—the one I'd been starting and stopping in my imagination all year long—had begun to play again. So Mom would be there to greet Dad after all, smiling and crying tears of joy just like Marmee would be in my shadow box. But then what? Why couldn't life be more like books, where you could read ahead and find out the end?

• • • • •

Operation Homecoming in the big gym at the rec center should have been renamed Operation Chaos. The organizers had rolled out long sheets of butcher paper on the floor and distributed buckets of markers so that we could get right to work on our creations. But anticipation in the air was so high that all the little kids had revved themselves into a hyperactive frenzy. With the doors open to the grills out back on the patio, it looked as if someone had set up a fog machine, and the kids ran screeching through the smoky gym with their fists clenched around markers and drippy Popsicles. Within fifteen minutes, the banner Nora and I had been making—WELCOME HOME SGT. WINNINGHAM! WE ♥ U—had three dusty shoeprints across it and a grape-colored splash right in the middle of our perfectly outlined heart.

Mom had been off chatting and trading hugs with a group of wives across the gym, but suddenly she was hurrying toward me, weaving through the buffet tables and throngs of stampeding kids. She thrust out her cell phone, practically shouting over the racket around us. "It's for you!"

I staggered up from the spot where I'd been kneeling and reached across our trampled banner for the phone. "Who is it?"

Mom mouthed something, but I couldn't tell what. I pressed the phone to my ear and hurried outside. "Hello?" I barked into the phone. "Hello?" By the time I had dodged my way around the grills and the condiment station and a noisy game of volleyball to a place under the trees where I could hear, Tucker was shouting too. "It's Tucker! Where are you? The circus?"

"Sort of," I said with a quivery laugh. "Sorry about that." I wandered over to the nearest maple tree and leaned against it. "I can hear you now."

"Hildy had your mom's number on her phone," Tucker said. "She wanted me to call you."

"She did?" Then I bit back my excitement. Maybe Tucker was only calling to make the message official. *Don't come back.*

"How's Hildy doing?" I asked carefully. "I still don't know what happened. Did she break her hip?"

"No, turns out she only bruised it. She keeps bragging about having the bones of a forty-year-old. But she sprained her ankle and her blood pressure kept shooting up, so the doctors made her stay in the hospital until they could get it back to normal."

"So she's home now?"

"Yep." Tucker exhaled. He sounded drained. "She got home a couple of days ago. Garrett built ramps to the stage and the front door for her wheelchair, but so far she's stayed in bed most of the time."

"Poor Hildy," I said softly. "I bet that's driving her crazy."

"Totally. She hates feeling useless. That's why I called. I think it would cheer her up if you came to see her."

I sagged deeper against the tree. "What about your dad? Is he still there?"

"No. Mine's been helping a ton and she talked him into going back to Des Moines yesterday."

"I'm really sorry, Tucker." I sat down in the nest of roots at my feet. "Your father started asking me all kinds of questions and I had to tell him that we weren't in the gym when Hildy had her accident. Did you get in huge trouble?"

I could hear Tucker's drawn-out sigh. "My dad did what he always does. Yelled and stomped around and then when I explained what we were doing—why we were looking at the mural—he freaked out all over again. But he calmed down eventually . . . like he always does," he repeated.

"You admitted we were trying to find the pearls?"

"Yeah. He thinks it's ridiculous. And I have to say I think it's pretty goofy myself, after all the time I wasted crawling around on Hildy's boat."

"What?" I let out a surprised laugh. "You did? Didn't Hugh tell you that we already looked there?"

"Yeah, but I thought I might as well give it a try too. Just in case. Anyway," he went on, "I think Hildy might have gotten wind that my dad gave you a hard time. She wants you to come over and visit her one day if you can."

"Of course I can come," I told him with a catch in my voice. "What about tomorrow?"

"Sure," Tucker said just as a rowdy cheer from the volleyball game came drifting through the trees. I smiled into the phone.

On my way back to the rec center, I spotted Mom standing on the lawn near the volleyball court, searching for me. Her face cleared as I came trotting out of the grove of maples. "I was worried," she called out. "What did Tucker say? Is everything all right with Hildy?"

I could see our welcome-home banner with its Popsicle stains rolled up under my mother's arm. She almost dropped it in surprise when I hurried over to hug her. "Everything's fine," I said as I rested my head against her chest.

Maybe Fourth of July wasn't so bad this year after all.

TWENTY-EIGHT

MY FIRST GLIMPSE of Hildy after her accident was so scary that I stood frozen on the stage like a bad actress struggling to remember my lines. The lighting probably made things worse. With the heavy velvet curtains shrouding all four sides and dark rafters where the ceiling should have been, the only brightness came from a few dim lamps scattered around the stage.

"I know, I know," Hildy said once I had floundered through my hello and taken a seat in the straight-back chair beside her bed. "I'm a mess." She reached up and patted her scalp and the sparse gray fluff that sprouted from it. Her skin matched her hair. Without makeup it was the color of ashes, and she looked more shrunken than ever, propped in the middle of her giant four-poster bed, swallowed in her robe and covers. "Bring me my wig, will you, Mine?" Hildy called. "Ren looks like she's about to faint."

Mine laughed and scooped the clump of stiff brown curls from the top of a dresser that sat in the corner. When she delivered it, Hildy plunked the wig on her head like a hat. Then she put on her glasses. "Better?" she asked.

I didn't know how to answer. Luckily Mine leaned over and gave the wig a couple of quick little tugs. "There," she said. "You look awesome." She moved the glass of water closer on Hildy's bedside table. "Need anything else?"

"No, dear. You've done enough this morning." Wincing, Hildy sank back against the pillows that were piled up behind her. "You go tend to Hugh. Ren will keep me company for a little while."

"Did you see Hugh when you came in?" Mine asked me.

"He and Tucker opened the door for me. They were headed out to the labyrinth. Sounds like it's almost done," I added brightly.

Hildy's expression turned bleak. "I told Garrett I wanted to be the first one down the path." She sighed. "But who knows how long that will take. You all will have to go ahead without me, I suppose."

I shot Mine a worried look. "The labyrinth will be good motivation for you, Hildy," Mine said. "The sooner you get back on your feet, the sooner you can get rid of this stuff." She picked up the walker and thumped it down next to the wheelchair at the end of the bed.

Hildy smiled wanly, closing her eyes like an obedient child.

"I'll be right next door in the kitchen," Mine told me as she stepped through the curtains at the front of the stage. Once Mine had gone, I glanced back to start a conversation with Hildy, but she had drifted off to sleep. I couldn't help staring for a few seconds, at her sunken cheeks, at the tiny blue veins in the hollows of her temples. Then I forced my gaze away and let it roam around the stage. There were Oriental rugs on the wooden floor and heavy antiques with doilies on top—like what you'd expect to see in an old woman's bedroom. Still, I couldn't help imagining that any minute the curtains might open, the lights would lift, and there, lined up below, would be the shadowy audience ready to watch us—Hildy and me—starring in our own little play.

I jumped when Hildy suddenly spoke up beside me in her husky voice. "Your dad will be home soon," she said.

"That's right." I smiled. "Only one more week."

"That's wonderful, honey. I bet you can hardly wait."

"I can't. But—" I knotted my fingers together in my lap. "But I'm scared too."

"Why's that?"

Was I really going to say it? Out loud? I took a deep breath in and then let it go, pushing my words free at the same time. "My dad moved out, right before he left for Afghanistan. All year I've been telling myself my parents will get back together as soon as my dad comes home. But now . . . I'm not so sure anymore."

"That's a bitter pill to swallow, isn't it?" Hildy's tone was so matter-of-fact, almost like she was talking to another grownup, that I glanced up in surprise.

"We can't hold back change, Ren," she said. "Sometimes things change for the better. Sometimes for the worse. Either way, we've got to be grateful for what we have and take life as it comes—good and bad—one step at a time."

I leaned forward, considering, and rested my chin on the heel of my hand. "It sounds pretty simple when you say it that way."

"Simple!" Hildy snorted and shook her head. "No, ma'am. Change is hard. If it were simple, would I be wearing this darn wig?"

We were still laughing when Hildy turned to look at something on the bedside table. At first I thought she might want a drink of water, but then I realized what she was gazing at—an old photograph propped against her lamp. It was the picture of her father and brother standing on the back of her dad's clamming boat—the same one she had tucked in her apron that morning when I had found her up on the balcony and confessed to opening the safe in the principal's office.

"Can I see?" I asked, reaching for the photo. Hildy nodded.

I peered down at the faces, searching for a family resemblance. "Your brother, Tom, was pretty cute," I said. "How old was he when this was taken?"

"Oh, probably twelve or thirteen. About Tucker's age. And yep, he was a looker, all right. The girls were crazy about him. They used to fight over whose books he would carry at school." I smiled. It sounded like Tucker and his great-uncle had a lot in common.

I tilted the photo into the lamplight. There was a name painted on the back of the boat, just underneath the spot where Tom and his father were standing. "Wait," I said suddenly. "I thought your dad's boat was called the *Little Miss*."

Hildy plucked at the collar of her robe in exasperation. "No, those fools that I hired to do that new paint job got it all wrong. Instead of doing what I told them, they went by what they could still read on the stern. They thought the 'Miss' stood for Mississippi and they completely left off the best part of her name. The word *Pearl* was the one closest to the waterline and it had worn completely away over the years."

"So your dad's boat was actually called *Little Miss Pearl*?"

"That's right, but everybody called her *Pearl* for short." She squirmed on her pillows, trying to find a comfortable spot. "By the time I discovered the mistake, Garrett had already hauled the boat into the gym. I was fit to be tied. She's older than me, that boat. Spent her whole life as *Pearl* until one bad paint job turned her into the silly *Little Miss*. I haven't gotten round to making them fix it yet, but it's on my to-do list."

Hildy let out a hoarse laugh and patted at her head. "What's wrong, honey? Why are you looking at me so funny? Is my hair crooked again?"

"Hildy, did Tucker ever tell you what he and I were doing that day when you fell? Hugh was with us too."

"No," she said, looking startled. "But I was wondering where the three of you ran off to so fast."

"We went to look at the mural," I said. "Mr. Bonnycastle's mural. We thought there might be a clue about where to find the pearls so we took the ladder out to the landing so we could climb up and see."

"The mural," Hildy repeated in awe. She pressed her hand to her cheek. "Of course, Bonny painted it! I should have thought of studying that old painting a long time ago." Her eyes widened behind her glasses. "Did you find anything?"

"We thought so . . . at first." I moved to the edge of her bed and carefully lowered myself down, making sure not to jostle the mattress. "Did you ever notice those boats in the painting?"

"Boats?" Hildy blinked. "There're two of them, right? I guess I never paid them much attention."

"Well, the one closest to the shore has a name written on its side. One word. Guess what it is?" I gave the photograph a little shake.

"Pearl!" Hildy cried. She had both hands pressed to her cheeks now, remembering. "Sometimes Pop let Tom take *Pearl* out to cruise the river on Sundays, and Bonny would go along. It was one of their favorite things to do together."

"But, Hildy—" I said. I needed to stop her before she got too excited. "We already searched your dad's boat. And I'm sorry, but the box . . . it's not there."

Hildy's eyes were blazing as she pushed herself up from the pillows. "Of course it is," she said. "You just didn't know where to look." Then all at once she was grabbing at her covers and throwing them aside. "Get me that wheelchair, Ren."

"Wait, Hildy! What are you doing?" I set the photo on the table and stood up, holding my hands out in a steadying motion. "Let me get Mine." I started backing away and then dashed for the curtains.

I only had to call Mine's name once before her frightened face appeared in the serving window. "You've got to come quick!" I yelled. "Hildy's trying to get up and I'm not sure if I can stop her."

Mine couldn't stop her either. "The gym?" she exclaimed, when she found out where Hildy wanted to go. "You've got to be kidding me, right? Don't get me wrong, Hildy, I think you've come a long way since the hospital, but you're not ready to get back to the museum yet."

The whole time Mine had been arguing, Hildy had been slowly but surely edging her tiny feet to the floor. She was wearing red socks and one ankle was wrapped tightly in an Ace bandage. With a loud sigh, she stopped and glared at us over the top of her glasses. "Listen, you two," she said. "If you don't bring me that wheelchair this minute, I'm going to crawl to the gym. Now which is it going to be?"

TWENTY-NINE

AT FIRST MINE DIDN'T TRY to ask any more questions about Hildy's mission. She was too preoccupied with transferring Hildy safely from her bed to her wheelchair and down the new ramp off the stage. Then halfway across the cafetorium, we spotted Hugh and Tucker in the kitchen.

"What are you guys up to?" Mine called.

Hugh came to the window, wiping his drippy chin on his arm. "We needed water," he said. "It's really hot out there. Hey, Hildy," he said, "can I have a ride on your wheelchair? Where are you guys going?"

"We're going to the gym," Hildy barked over her shoulder as Mine kept pushing her toward the hallway. "No wheelchair rides, but you better come along. I'm going to need somebody about your size."

Mine chuckled drily. "Come on, Hildy." She looked over at me. "Ren? The suspense is killing me. What's going on?"

I opened my mouth, trying to figure out where to start. As far as I knew, Hugh hadn't told his mother a thing about the pearls. But before I could answer, Hugh came running up behind us in the hall. "You need somebody my size?" he asked as he trotted along beside Hildy's wheelchair. "How come?"

Then I heard a sloshing noise, and when I looked back Tucker was there too with Garrett's water jug swinging at his side. "What's up?" he panted, nudging my arm.

"Hush, everybody," Hildy ordered, as Mine rolled her through the foyer. "That's enough questions. I've been waiting most of my life to figure this out. If you're lucky, you've only got to wait about five more minutes."

We all fell quiet, but when we trailed through the doors to the gym and Hildy told Mine to steer her over to the boat, Tucker couldn't keep silent anymore. "I thought so!" he burst out. "This is about the pearls, isn't it?" He whipped around to face me. "Ren, didn't you tell her we already looked? Give it up, will you?"

I shrugged in desperation. "I did tell her, Tucker! I—"

"Hold your horses now, Tucker." Hildy signaled for Mine to turn her wheelchair around. "I'm grateful to Ren for being so persistent. I should have thought of looking at the mural ages ago, but I didn't. And it never occurred to me to look on Pop's boat either. Not until Ren kicked this rusty brain of mine into gear and I remembered the hiding place."

"Hiding place?" Tucker squinted in confusion. "What hiding place?"

Hildy crossed her arms over her bathrobe. "Well, maybe I could show you if you'd stop interrupting for a half second." She was teasing, but not really. Tucker clamped his mouth shut.

"Go on, Hugh," Hildy said once we were finally gathered at the boat. "Climb up."

Hugh hopped up on the platform and practically vaulted himself inside. Then he stood grinning down at us, bouncing on his toes and waiting for more instructions.

"See that bench in the stern?" Hildy squawked up at Hugh. I felt my face fall. *The bench.* Hugh gave me a worried look, but he didn't say anything. He went to the opposite end of the boat like he was told and we all followed. Mine rolled Hildy right up to the stern.

"There's a lid on the bench," Hildy called. "Open it."

I glanced back at Tucker. Now he was the one folding his arms. "I already looked in there," he said under his breath.

"Shhh," I scolded.

The hinges of the bench let out their rusty squeak.

"Now climb in and kneel down," Hildy told Hugh.

I gripped the wooden side of the boat, standing on my tiptoes and craning my neck to see, but I wasn't quite tall enough to get a good view. Hugh's head disappeared and then he popped up again. "Did you know it smells like fish in here, Hildy?"

"Of course it does." Hildy laughed. "That's one thing the new paint job couldn't get rid of. Now, Hugh," she called. "Once you're down in there, look toward the stern where the motor would be. You see that little wall at the back of the bench?"

There was no answer. I couldn't stand it anymore. "Hugh?" I yelled. "Do you see the wall at the back of the bench?"

Hugh's muffled voice came floating out from under the lid. "Yeah?"

Tucker pressed in beside me, and now Mine was standing on her tiptoes too.

We all turned to Hildy. She clutched the arms of her wheelchair. "Tell him there's a tiny notch at the top of that wall. He needs to get hold of the notch and pull. There're spring hinges on the other side." I hoisted myself over the side of the boat and then crouched next to the bench, repeating Hildy's instructions.

"There's no notch," Hugh wailed up at me. When he poked his head out this time, his hair was damp with sweat and his cheeks were flushed. "What is a notch, anyway?"

"Seriously, Hildy," Mine said with the first hint of impatience in her voice. "What exactly is Hugh supposed to be looking for?"

"Pop's secret compartment," Hildy cried, thumping her fist on the arm of her wheelchair. My pulse quickened. *So there was a secret compartment after all.*

"I don't mean to be rude here," Mine said, "but what would an old workboat like this be doing with a secret compartment inside?"

"Pop made it," Hildy told her, like it was the most obvious thing in the world. "When the shells around Fortune ran out, he had to go looking for shell beds farther away. Sometimes he'd be gone for days, working at camps full of strangers up and down the Mississippi. Pop had a mortal fear of getting robbed. If he made a few dollars or found a pearl or two, he wanted a safe place to stash them. After all that work, he wasn't about to come home empty-handed."

Hugh had disappeared inside the bench again while Hildy had been talking. Now she folded her hands in her lap. "He'll find it," she said, nodding to herself. "It's there."

She seemed so sure. But all the same, when I heard Hugh's little whoop of delight and he crawled from the bowel of the boat holding a square package wrapped in waxy brown cloth and string, I could barely believe it. Hugh seemed just as astonished. No one said a word as I handed the package down to Tucker, who hurried over to place it in his grandmother's outstretched hands.

When she fumbled with the string, Tucker pulled out his pocketknife to help. Then we all crowded around Hildy's wheelchair as she pulled away the wrapping with shaking hands and opened the lid of the small pine box underneath.

Hugh was the first one to speak. "They're glowing," he whispered. He was right. The pearls glowed, and Hildy's face shone with tears. She reached into the shimmering pile and pulled out the largest. It was almost perfectly round and the color was even prettier than I had imagined—a deep dusky pink—the color of sunsets.

I heard Mine let out a little gasp beside me. "No way," she marveled. "Did that come out of the Mississippi?"

"Indeed it did," Hildy said as she lifted the Blushing Beauty into the light. It didn't look like anything you'd expect to find on the bottom of the Mississippi, or the floor of a barroom, or the bottom of an old wooden boat. "At last," Hildy murmured. "My brother, Tom, can rest in peace."

THIRTY

MOM LET ME MISS CHURCH the next morning so I could ride out to the school early. I wanted to beat the heat and be there before all the excitement started. As soon as Mayor Joy had laid eyes on Hildy's pearls and heard the story of how they were lost and found again, he called his friend and fellow-mayor over in Bellefield to tell him the amazing tale. And within hours, two newspaper reporters and a television crew had gathered on the steps of the school, hoping to get the scoop on the Blushing Beauty and the unusual new tourist attraction that was being created in the forgotten town of Fortune.

As Wayne grazed nearby, Mayor Joy had politely declined to comment "at the present time." But he invited the reporters to return the next day when Hildy Baxter, the founder of the Fortune Pearl Button Museum, and other local officials would be taking questions at an afternoon press conference.

Apparently Hildy wasn't going to be selling her treasure anytime soon. "Absolutely not," the mayor of Bellefield had advised her. "With those pearls on display, you'll have more publicity and funding for the museum than you'll know what to do with."

But for now the school was still quiet. It stood silent and imposing in the soft morning light, as if it was gathering strength for the changes that were coming. Once I parked my bike, I ran through the dew-covered grass, breathing a grateful sigh when I rounded the corner and looked out at the labyrinth. No one was there. I'd have it all to myself.

I moved slowly to the entrance—about where home plate used to be—and looked out over the paths lined with knee-high walls of shells. Last night when I finally searched the word on the Internet, I had learned that labyrinth-walking was supposed to make you feel peaceful. The Labyrinth Society Web site even listed something called the "365 Day Club," where members pledge to walk through a labyrinth every day for one year. "Daily walkers report the labyrinth has become a part of their being," the site said, "bringing a sense of peace to all aspects of their lives." It seemed impossible, even kind of silly, but at the same time I was suddenly desperate to give it a try. These days my mind never stopped swimming with questions—about Mom and Dad, Hildy and the museum, Tucker, junior high . . .

If a walk through some shells could ease my worries a little, why not? I squared my shoulders, blew out a big breath of air, and stepped onto the path.

To be honest, I felt embarrassed at first, strolling round and round with my hands clasped behind my back like stiff Mr. Vanderveer from the historical society. I scanned the windows of the school. What if someone was watching? Tucker was probably waiting for me. I had told him I'd be there early so I could help with setting up the display case for the pearls before the press conference.

Stop it, I told myself. According to the Web, I was supposed to keep my mind quiet as I walked and concentrate on rhythmic, gentle breathing. *Feel the sun and breeze on your skin,* one site said. *The soil under your feet.*

There actually was a little breeze. I could hear the corn rustling and the throaty whistle of a red-winged blackbird off near Mayor Joy's place. I tried forcing my eyes to stay on the path, but they kept straying to the little walls of shells on both sides and all those thousands of button holes, made by hundreds of button-cutters over the years.

Concentrate on the placement of one foot in front of the other. I stared down at the dirt path and realized what I was looking at—wheelchair tracks and the imprints of Garrett's giant work boots. I smiled to myself. So maybe

Hildy had been the first one to christen the labyrinth after all.

I kept spiraling slowly, adding my tracks to Hildy's and Garrett's, until all at once I was there, in the middle of the labyrinth. *Pause on reaching the center. Surrender your burdens.* I closed my eyes and saw the four of us—Mom, Dad, Nora, and me—sitting on a blanket by the river, eating my special brownies that Dad had ordered. Blue was there too, waiting in the truck behind us, because after the picnic, Dad and I would take him for a ramble in the woods and then I'd go back to Dad's new place to spend the night. That might be kind of fun, I thought, having a sleepover with just my father and Old Blue.

"Hi, Ren!"

I glanced up from my surrendering. Hugh was standing at the entrance waving wildly as if I'd been lost on a desert island. "Stay there!" he called. "I'm coming in!"

I wondered what the Labyrinth Society would think of Hugh's walking style. He started out with his head down, moving speedily along the pathway like he was Mr. Pac-Man. But then his jerky little march turned into a jog, and about halfway to the middle he made his arms into airplane wings. By the time he reached the last spiral, he was shuffling.

"Is this your first time through?" I asked when he joined me at the center.

"Uh-huh. Garrett made us wait for Hildy. The pearls

tired her out so much that she wasn't ready to come out here until after dinner last night."

"Garrett pushed her in the wheelchair?"

"Yeah, and then the mosquitoes came out and it got kind of dark, so Mine said I should wait till this morning. She said the vibe would be better without the bugs and a flashlight."

I laughed. "So what do you think of the vibe so far?"

"Pretty good." Hugh shrugged. He surveyed the little circle of open space at our feet. "You think it's okay if we sit down?"

"I think so," I said. I didn't remember reading anything on the labyrinth sites that said "No Sitting Allowed."

When Hugh splayed across the labyrinth's center, I told him it might be better if we sat in a yoga sort of pose, so we ended up side by side, facing the school, with our legs crisscrossed in front of us.

"Can you believe it, Hugh?" I asked as we sat gazing across the field of shells at the school. "We did it. We're the Fortune Hunters."

Hugh grinned, squinting one eye and peering at the sun coming over the tower. "Now we *have* to carve our names up there."

"We will," I assured him. "As soon as there's a new rail for me to hold onto. And no more wasps."

"I already asked Garrett about fixing the tower and

he said he'd work on it. But he's got to hurry up and do it before Tucker has to go home." Hugh was quiet for a second. "And before I have to go back to Chicago."

"What?" My chest squeezed with dismay. "What do you mean, go back to Chicago?"

"Mine says we're probably moving back there once Hildy's all better."

"But . . . but I thought Mine liked it here. She's made friends with Hildy and she's gotten so much better at cooking. And I thought you liked it too."

"I do!" Hugh said. "I like lots of stuff. You and Hildy and Garrett. And Wayne. I'm his second favorite person now besides the Mayor. And Sister Loud wants to keep giving me piano lessons, and I like my bunk bed and the card catalog, and I'm even starting to think buttons are interesting." Hugh stopped and dug in his pocket for his button blank. "You still got yours?" he asked.

I shook my head. "No, I think I've learned that I might be better off making my own luck from now on."

Hugh studied the button blank cupped in his palm. "Part of me really wants to stay here," he said in a faraway voice. "But when everybody's busy or gone, it gets kind of lonely, you know?" I couldn't answer. Then I felt his hand on my arm, delicate as a leaf.

"I'm going to miss you, Hugh," I said, trying to swallow the ache in my throat.

"I'll come and visit sometimes."

I nodded. They were the same words I had said to him about a month ago. It seemed like years had passed since then. "I know you will," I told him.

I traced my finger through one of Hildy's wheelchair tracks near my knee. What was it she had told me yesterday on the stage? Something about taking life and changes as they come—good and bad—one step at a time.

"You ready to walk back out?" I asked.

"Just a second." Hugh leaned over to the nearest up-turned shell and carefully placed his button blank inside its pearly hollow, covering one of the holes that had been cut so long ago. "Okay, I'm ready," he said as he pushed himself to his feet.

Then, with a little bow, he swept his hand forward. "Ladies first."

I bowed back and stepped onto the path.

AUTHOR'S NOTE

·····

The idea for this book began more than ten years ago, about 1,500 miles from the Iowa banks of the Mississippi. I was vacationing with my family on Captiva Island in Florida, and one rainy day we found ourselves at the Bailey-Matthews National Shell Museum in nearby Sanibel. I remember following behind my three young daughters as they flitted around the exhibits, marveling over record-size conch shells and other exotic specimens from the deep waters of Florida and the Caribbean. Then, just as the girls had hit their museum limit and were pulling me toward the door, I spotted a shell punched with holes in one of the display cases. The label underneath mentioned Muscatine, Iowa. Until that moment, I had no idea that buttons were once made from shells or that the former

"Pearl Button Capital of the World" was only a forty-five-minute drive from my adopted home in Iowa City.

For me, like most people, the Midwest had always meant farm country. So I was fascinated when I made my first visit to the Muscatine History and Industry Center and learned about the brief stretch of time during the early 1900s when Iowa was more famous for its harvest of freshwater shells than its production of corn and soybeans. My original visit to the Center was full of interesting surprises: in 1911, for example, there were so many children under fourteen working in Muscatine's pearl button factories that they formed their own union; Ronald Reagan, when he was still an actor, thirty-five years before he became president of the United States, had had the honor of selecting Muscatine's Pearl Button Queen; buttons made from shell feel cold to the touch compared to those made from plastic; and most exciting of all, some clammers made their fortune by finding pearls inside the humble-looking shells that they dragged from the river.

Though the field trip to Muscatine had captured my imagination, I was preoccupied with another book project at the time. I tucked the History and Industry Center brochure into my "Idea File" and soon forgot about it. Then, a few years later, I stumbled across an article in the *Des Moines Register* called "Fading Away." The piece told the story of Le Roy, the smallest incorporated town left in Iowa. Population: 13. According to the article, the street signs were falling down. The sidewalks were overgrown. But the town still had a mayor—a seventy-one-year-old man named Emmet Joy who happened to own an outspoken donkey named Wayne and who still conducted city-council meetings in an old hog-weighing station.

On a whim, I tracked down Mayor Joy's phone number and asked if I could come for a visit. I'd always been intrigued by modern-day ghost towns like Le Roy. On countless car trips through different states, I had seen lonely old main streets with shuttered buildings flash by, and I could never help wondering: Who had lived there once and who on earth would want to stick around? Now was my chance to hear some of those stories firsthand.

By the time I met Mayor Joy at his farm on the out-skirts of town, Wayne had sadly passed away and two more people had moved out of Le Roy, continuing a trend that had started when the railroad stopped running there in 1946. Once we were finished chatting, the mayor said I should go see the old brick school. It had closed in 1981, but someone had recently bought it for $3,500. The first tenants, a young family, had moved into a corner of the building where the school offices used to be. "Just bang on the door and holler," the mayor told me. "They'll let you in." Luckily they did, and driving home that day I thought back to my discoveries in Muscatine, and the fictional town of Fortune began to take shape in my mind.

While Muscatine managed to survive the rise and fall

of the pearl-button industry, other former button towns scattered along our country's rivers—from Minnesota to Tennessee—disappeared with the changing times, leaving barely a trace. I wrote this book in the hope that it will encourage curious readers to always be on the lookout for the Mayor Joys and Hildys of the world, who keep our fading history alive.

A typical family-run clamming camp along the banks of the Mississippi, circa 1915. While men worked the shell beds, women and children set up camp, cooked meals, and kept the fires burning under the metal tanks where the mussels would be steamed open and prepared for cleaning. (Courtesy of the Arnold Miller Photograph Collection, Musser Public Library, Muscatine, Iowa)

Father and son with cut-shell pile, circa 1940. Like the character of Tom, many boys worked alongside their fathers on clamming boats. Others were put to work onshore, hauling buckets of shells and sorting them according to size before the cutting process. (Courtesy of the Muscatine History and Industry Center)

The cutting shop at the U.S. Button Company, circa 1915.
Shell-cutting was a dangerous business that required skill, as
well as patience with unpleasant working conditions. As jets
of water sprayed over their machinery to control heat, dust,
and flying bits of debris, the cutters held each shell in place
with tongs and used tubular saws to produce the blanks.
(Courtesy of the Muscatine History and Industry Center)

Cut shells alongside a pile of pearl buttons—the finished product. Once the pearl buttons had been drilled with holes and polished, they were hand-sewn onto decorative cards for display in retail shops. Button companies often hired out the sewing to local families, who completed the work at home. (Courtesy of the Copeland Collection)

Muscatine's Pearl Button Queen, 1946. Thirty-five years before he became president, actor Ronald Reagan was given the honor of selecting the queen from seven contestants. In a 1981 *Muscatine Journal* interview, Helen Burke recalled what it was like to be chosen: "They gave me a big bunch of roses and put a crown on my head—and I immediately fainted!" (Courtesy of the Muscatine History and Industry Center)

ACKNOWLEDGMENTS

• • • • •

If there were such a thing as a "Kind and Gracious Fellow-Author Award," Jeffrey Copeland should win it. Jeff patiently answered my countless questions about the pearl-button industry, reviewed my manuscript, shared photographs, and provided all-around encouragement, even though I had an uncanny knack for contacting him on the eve of his own book tours and research trips. His fine book *Shell Games: The Life and Times of Pearl McGill, Industrial Spy and Pioneer Labor Activist* (Paragon House, 2012) served as an important resource in my research.

My sincere appreciation also goes to:

Melanie K. Alexander for her invaluable pictorial history, *Muscatine's Pearl Button Industry*, Images of America Series (Arcadia Publishing, 2007).

Mike Kilen, *Des Moines Register* reporter, for his feature story "Fading Away" (October 12, 2008), which helped to inspire this story and provided my first introduction to Mayor Emmet Joy.

Mary Wildermuth, director of the Muscatine History and Industry Center, for her assistance with my research and photo selection.

Terry Eagle, assistant director of the Center, for guiding one of the best field trips of my writing career. I'll never forget my frozen-in-time look inside the old button factory, as well as the tour of the McKee Button Company, still in operation more than a century after its founding.

Margaret Weber—also more than one hundred years old!—for sharing her memories of the Weber Button Company.

My dear friends and colleagues Terri Gullickson and Jennifer Black Reinhardt, as always, for their support and honest opinions.

I'm also grateful to Laura Langlie, my wonderful agent, for having faith when mine was wavering . . . and to my wise editor, Margaret Ferguson, for helping me to grind and polish my rough button blank into a pearlier version of its former self.

My deepest thanks I've saved for Bobby and Dan Ray for tirelessly listening, reading, and smoothing the way.